"Ostensibly, Woiwode weaves a tender, slow-burning story of death, grief, and rebirth, but really, it's her intoxicating love-letter descriptions of a windswept North Dakotan prairie and its inhabitants that will sweep you off your feet. A moving tale about the resilience of family relationships and the power of memory, *Past Darkness* unravels a tale, brimming with love and hope, to prove it."

Elissa Elliott, author, *Eve: A Novel*

"Beautifully haunting, sublime yet profound, Laurel Woiwode's debut novel is the truest of romances: the romance between the individual soul and the Father's persistent love and healing."

John L. Moore, author, *The Breaking of Ezra Riley* and *Bitter Roots*

"A profound story of sudden, devastating loss and the tenuous, graceful process of healing and redemption. The characters who move through this powerful first novel are as complex or nuanced as the people who move through our lives; you will remember Gabrielle Larson, Uncle Will, Aunt Bea, and Ian Mackenzie long after you turn the final page. You will remember the places they inhabit as well. Woiwode evokes rural North Dakota with the tender confidence that comes only when a writer knows the shape of a place as well as she knows the shape of her hand. From one lucid sentence to the next, she illuminates the intimate mysteries of the natural world, and invites us to share in its expansive beauty."

Karen Halvorsen Schreck, author, *While He Was Away* and *Sing for Me*

"Woiwode's story is moving and elegantly framed, capturing the pain, growth, and development of an individual's heart, mind, and soul. It is a rare sort of story in our world today, but Woiwode succeeds in crafting this individual against the great expanse of North Dakota, interweaving the geography of the state with her central character's awakening."

Michael Brandon Lopez, lawyer

"A wonderful story of hope, faith, and forgiveness. And also courage—to face our fears and overcome them."

Annette Haas, veterinarian

PAST
DARKNESS

A NOVEL

PAST
DARKNESS

LAUREL WOIWODE

::: CROSSWAY

WHEATON, ILLINOIS

Past Darkness: A Novel

Copyright © 2013 by Laurel Woiwode

Published by Crossway
   1300 Crescent Street
   Wheaton, Illinois 60187

Cover design: Josh Dennis

Cover image: Shutterstock

First printing 2013

Printed in the United States of America

Trade paperback ISBN: 978-1-4335-3518-5
PDF ISBN: 978-1-4335-3519-2
Mobipocket ISBN: 978-1-4335-3520-8
ePub ISBN: 978-1-4335-3521-5

Library of Congress Cataloging-in-Publication Data
Woiwode, Laurel.
Past darkness / Laurel Woiwode.
  p. cm.
  ISBN 978-1-4335-3518-5 (tp)
1. Parents—Death—Fiction. 2. Loss (Psychology)—Fiction. I. Title.
PS3623.O48P37   2013
813'.6—dc23   2012028029

Crossway is a publishing ministry of Good News Publishers.

BP		22	21	20	19	18	17	16	15	14	13
15	14	13	12	11	10	9	8	7	6	5	4	3	2	1

For Dad and Mom
Who always believe

I have been one acquainted with the night.
I have walked out in rain—and back in rain.
I have outwalked the furthest city light.
Robert Frost

The light shines in the darkness,
and the darkness has not overcome it.
John 1:5

Chapter
1

I started listening again to the radio, to a counseling program, and realized people can't be objective about their lives. Almost every story is subjective, after all, and each life lived is a story. The stories I heard people tell on the radio sounded wild and fantastic, but I was inclined to believe them. Perhaps because my own story sometimes seems made up.

My parents were both musicians, but they came to music in different ways. My mother was from a Norwegian immigrant community that settled on the plains of the Dakotas. She had a gift for music, especially piano. Her parents encouraged her to pursue this talent, and she went to study music at Wheaton College, west of Chicago.

At about the same time, my father was pre-law at the University of Illinois. He was the oldest of a large family, and his father expected him to take over the family firm, which dealt primarily in the growing and lucrative business of divorce. Dad started playing the guitar as a defense against his disillusionment with an increasingly litigious society. His father hated musicians.

One of my father's friends introduced him to the Cornerstone festival, not far from Chicago, which featured prominent speakers and musicians. Even though it was a Christian event, the friend convinced Dad to attend because of the music. The festival people accepted Dad without judgment, and he became a Christian. He left the university, unable to keep up the pretense that he was meant to be a lawyer. He began working for the Cornerstone ministry, and met my mother when she volunteered there. She told me she'd never met such an enthusiastic, talented musician. They began their own music ministry after they were married.

This is a little background for my story, which begins in medias res, when I was fifteen. I was an only child who thrived on Chicago life, even though we lived in the suburbs. I attended Christian Liberty Academy in Arlington Heights and enjoyed my classes and the time I got to spend with my circle of friends.

I did wonder if my parents wanted a boy instead of a girl. My name, Gabrielle, was pronounced Gay-bri-ELLE, closer to the male version, and not GAB-ri-EL-la, the usual for a girl. It didn't bother me, but it made me sit down and think at times.

As I got older, my parents let me sing with them during a few of their performances. I grew up with music—Mom sang to me and Dad played his compositions for me—and as I learned about music my goal was to enthrall an audience.

One evening, we drove up to the front entrance of an auditorium that had a sign announcing:

> The captivating husband-and-wife duo
> Introducing their daughter, Gabrielle Larson

"Where's the picture?" I said. "They're supposed to have our picture!"

"They'll see what we look like soon enough," Dad said, and turned off the car. "Are you ready?"

"Wait a minute," Mom said, and straightened his shirt collar.

I helped carry our instruments and sound equipment inside, and then parted the curtains from backstage and looked into the auditorium. I felt cold and sweaty as I stared at all the people there, since this was my first large event. We spent some time warming up, but we were introduced before my nerves settled. I sang harmony most of the night, waiting for my solo toward the end of the program.

"You are all in for a special treat tonight," Dad said into the microphone. "Not only do you get to hear one of my favorite hymns, but you get to hear one of my favorite people sing it!"

Dad started picking the melody on his guitar, and the audience's spreading stillness settled into me. I began singing with a clear voice: "This is my Father's world, and to my listening ears all nature sings, and round me rings the music of the spheres."

I started thinking about the people listening to me, and my voice broke. I could feel the burn of a blush spread over me from my forehead to fingertips, and I finished the song in a faint voice. I was silent until we reached home.

"I *never* want to do that again!"

"Oh, now Gabe, don't be too hard on yourself," Dad said. "You should have seen some of the mistakes I made when I started out. Like the time I started playing a song in the wrong key. I was like, 'Dude, what's up?' but I was so nervous, I didn't know what was wrong for a while."

"I'm serious!"

"I know how you feel, honey," Mom said. "But you know what they say about falling off a horse, right?"

I rolled my eyes, but she continued. "Why don't you come to the church program tomorrow to listen, and see how you feel then."

"Fine."

"That's m'girl," Dad said, and gave me a thumbs-up.

The next evening, I tried to imagine I'd never heard my parents sing. Mom's soprano and Dad's high baritone voices blended in a beautiful combination. For the finale they sang "I Know That My Redeemer Lives" from Handel's *Messiah*. It brought tears to my eyes, and I desired that power.

I wanted to do another solo, so I went through Mom's music until I found one I liked. I told her I wanted to learn the piece.

"I don't know, Gabe," she said. "It's difficult."

"I can do it."

"Honey, I don't want you to strain your voice."

I pulled the music out of her hands. "I want to do this song."

"All right," she said, looking almost afraid.

They scheduled me to sing at their next concert, so I practiced until my throat hurt, but I ignored the pain. My solo didn't go the way I planned. My voice didn't crack, but because the melody was fast and high, my enunciation wasn't clear and my voice had hardly any volume or depth.

I went backstage and fought back tears of frustration. *I practiced so hard! And for what? Nothing.*

"Gabrielle? Are you okay?" Dad was looking at me, his guitar suspended over its case.

"Yes."

"Look, I know you're disappointed in the way you sang," he said. "You know, harder isn't always better when it comes to music. Sometimes the best, most beautiful music is unbelievably simple." He smiled at me. "You have a beautiful voice, Gabe. Let people hear it."

I managed to nod.

"You have to let your voice mature before you put too much strain on it," Mom said.

I nodded again.

With practice, and with my parents' guidance, my voice improved and I began singing more often. And I let the praise I received—and began to expect—go to my head, I'm afraid.

My friends at school were annoyed because all I talked about was music and singing and how much fun I had performing. My

12

best friend, Carmen, who was always exuberant, was excited to hear about my singing. Even when some of my other friends stopped hanging out with me, Carmen didn't. However, one day at school, after I'd been talking all through lunchbreak about learning a new song, I noticed that Carmen was silent.

"Carmen," I said, "is everything okay?"

"Yeah, sure," she said.

"Uh, I think something's wrong."

Carmen looked at me, as if trying to decide whether to speak.

"Please, tell me. I'm your friend!"

"You haven't been much of one, Gabrielle."

"What?"

"All you do is talk about yourself. It's like you don't care about anyone else. There's stuff going on in my life too, you know? But you're acting like you're the only one that matters."

"That's just stupid," I said.

Carmen looked away and took a sip of her juice.

"What exactly do you mean, anyway?" I said.

Carmen slid her fork around until I wanted to slap her hand. "I was sent to the principal's office yesterday," she said.

"That's my fault?"

She looked at me and shook her head. "I yelled at someone, defending you."

"Well, I never asked you to do that," I said.

"That's not the point," Carmen said.

I was starting to feel uncomfortable. "Then what is?"

"You're being selfish," she said.

I didn't know what to say. I was shocked that I hadn't noticed until now how upset Carmen was.

"I'm sorry, Carmen," I said. "I didn't mean to act like that. I guess I got excited about singing, but, whatever, I'm sorry."

"Yeah, okay," Carmen said. She shrugged and looked at me. "I'm sure performing is exciting."

She stood up and picked up her food tray. I did the same.

"Yes, but still," I said. "I'm really sorry."

Carmen smiled but didn't say anything.

We slid our trays onto the counter where they were collected.

"I'm glad you finally said something to me," I said.

"Well, you are my best friend, Gabe."

"And you're mine, Carmen," I said, and hugged her. "I'm glad you didn't start ignoring me or something!"

"Hey, it was tempting!" Carmen grinned at me, and bounced on her toes.

"So, what *is* new with you?" I asked.

Carmen tried to look serious for a minute, then grinned and ran down the hallway toward her next class. She spun around, running backwards, and said, "Oh, you know, same ole same ole!"

I laughed as I watched her slip around a corner and out of sight.

I went home that day feeling loaded down with homework and guilt, even though Carmen had forgiven me.

I stepped into the kitchen at home and dropped my backpack on the floor. I heard music from the living room and remembered that Mom was away at some sort of women's group meeting, but Dad was home, sick with the flu. I poured myself some juice and opened the door to the living room. Dad was sprawled in an easy chair wearing sweatclothes and a flannel bathrobe, his head laid against the back of the chair. His eyes were closed, and his face looked feverish and his nose raw.

The strains of Vivaldi's *The Four Seasons* reverberated through the room—"Autumn" or "Winter," I couldn't remember which. One of Dad's hands lifted off the armrest and floated back and forth through the air as though he were conducting. The strings went through a phrase of stutter-like crescendos, overlapping each other, until the soloist's violin rose above them in a sweet roll of trills that traveled in an effortless slide up and down through several octaves. I could feel the vibrations of the contrabass and cellos in my chest. The violin solo continued, becoming eerie, breathy, and high-pitched, until all the strings joined into the same wild, raw, and stuttering crescendo, then faded in harmony. The hair rose on my arms.

Dad smiled, eyes still closed. A violent sneeze jerked him up and his eyes opened. He looked at me and smiled.

"How was school?" he asked, his voice hoarse.

I put my hand over his forehead. "It was fine." I knew I could mention Carmen, but didn't. "Do you feel any better?"

He shrugged. "I don't know, maybe."

Goosebumps still covered my arms, but Dad's forehead was hot and dry under my palm.

"Would you like some tea?" I asked.

He smiled again and I saw the weariness in his eyes. I wanted to make him feel better.

"I would love some," he said, and I could move again.

One day during the following week, I walked home from school, oblivious to the other students. *Trevor likes me!* I thought.

I did my homework, once at home, not caring if I did it well or not. When I was done, I went to the kitchen and sat on the counter, and watched Mom prepare dinner. I was sitting there, humming and drinking tea, when Mom looked at me and smiled.

"You sure are cheerful tonight. Any special reason?"

"No," I said. "Well, maybe."

"What might that be?" Mom said, as if to herself.

"Well, there's this guy—"

"Ah."

"What?"

"I didn't say anything."

"Mm-hmm, whatever. Well, anyway, he's really cool and his name is Trevor."

"So Trevor is cool?"

It didn't sound good when she said it.

"Yeah, he's cool. And one of his friends says Trevor likes me."

Mom smiled again, but it was a smile that excluded me. "Did his friend happen to say why this Trevor likes you?"

"No, I guess not. But does it matter? You don't seem happy. I thought you'd be happy if I was happy."

"Well, perhaps we should save our enthusiasm to see if anything comes of it." She shook out some lettuce as she spoke, emphasizing *enthusiasm* with a cascade of water droplets. I mumbled something incoherent.

"Pardon?"

"Maybe you won't be *enthusiastic* no matter what happens," I said.

Mom stopped tearing the lettuce leaves. "Gabrielle, you are very young to be getting involved with boys, and I don't know anything, good, bad, or otherwise, about this Trevor."

The reasonable tone of her voice made me angry.

"That's just an excuse!" I said. "You want to keep me as your little Gabrielle. I won't stay a little girl forever, and you can't make me!"

Dad walked in and looked at me in surprise.

"Gabe," he said, "don't talk to your mother like that."

"Of course you'd take *her* side!" I said.

His eyes widened. "*Gabrielle!* What's wrong with you?"

Tears gathered in my eyes as I pushed past him and out of the kitchen. I ran to my room and slammed the door. I slid down the wall in the corner, my anger spent.

I heard a knock on my door. I was too ashamed to respond. From between my arms, which were covering my face, I saw the door open and Dad's bare feet approach me. I was trying to avoid his face, so I focused on his toes. His big toenails were squarer than the others and dark hair curled over the knuckles of all ten of his toes. I wanted to point it out to him so we could laugh about it together, but I couldn't say anything. He stopped in front of me.

"Gabrielle?"

I saw his toes dig into the carpet as he squatted in front of me. He ran his hand over my hair. I shivered. He knelt and took me into his arms.

"I'm sorry I yelled, Gabrielle." His voice echoed through his chest into my ear. "Even though you were wrong to yell at Mom, I made it worse by yelling at you. Forgive me?"

I nodded, my head rubbing against his collarbone.

Dad held me tighter for a moment and then stood. "Do you want to go and talk to your mother?"

"No!" I said. "I can't talk to her yet."

Dad sat down on my bed and patted it for me to sit beside him. "Why not, Gabrielle?" he asked.

"Too ashamed."

"Ah, yes. Well, I know from experience that delay doesn't make apologizing easier. It just prolongs the inevitable, giving you more time to torment yourself." He rocked me from side to side with his arm that was over my shoulders. "Would it be better if she came here?" he asked.

"I guess."

"Don't be glum, dear, confession is good for the soul! Didn't somebody say that?" He squeezed me again, stood, and pointed to the doorway and deepened his voice.

"I go into the unknown, to bring the fair damsel Katherine to your side!" He trotted down the hall. I heard Mom's surprised shriek as he picked her up—"Don't carry me!" she cried—and came back. Mom was flushed and laughing as he stopped in front of my door and set her down.

"Your destination," he said, and bowed. Mom curtsied to him before he turned and went toward the kitchen. I had been laughing, but when Mom turned to me, smiling, my shame came back. I hid my face on her shoulder.

"I'm sorry," I said. "I'm stupid. I didn't mean any of those things."

She hugged me and rocked from side to side. "I forgive you, Gabrielle, of course I do," she said.

I felt like crying, but I laughed instead. Dad was singing what sounded like a madrigal, something about maidens fair and a feast to share and the toil not to be spared.

Mom laughed, the sound passing through her chest and into me before it reached my ears.

Chapter
2

I was in my room on a Friday evening, finishing homework so I'd be free for the rest of the weekend. I went to get some tea after finishing my algebra assignment, and stopped in the dark hall outside the kitchen door, out of my parents' sight, because I heard a serious tone in Dad's voice.

"Kate, I don't know. It seems like we never have quite enough bookings to make the advertising and instruments worthwhile." He sighed, and I heard him rattling in the dishpan. He seemed to be taking out his frustration on some silverware.

"There will always be dry spells," Mom said, and in another voice, "don't you think?"

"This seems more like a drought."

"I could go back to teaching full-time instead of subbing, Daniel."

"You were miserable when you had to put up with the politics in that school every day. And those little gremlins never gave you a moment's peace."

"True. But after all, I can put up with you!"

"Ha, ha, funny," Dad said. "Okay, joking aside, I'm starting to think maybe we're not doing the right thing here. I mean, we're barely making ends meet. And we should be putting money away for Gabrielle's college."

I could feel my face growing warm. *Were they thinking of quitting the music business? And for my sake?*

Dad's voice was quiet, so I leaned forward. I could see him standing at the sink, hands in the water, head bent over his chest. "I feel like a failure."

Mom set down the plate she'd been drying. "Daniel, look at me," she said. She pulled him to face her, his hands dripping soap and water. She gripped his biceps and shook him until he looked at her.

"Don't be absurd," she said. His head jerked back in surprise. "Daniel, you're the kindest and best man I ever met, and I'd still think the same and still love you as much as I do, even if we were living in a cardboard box!" She gave him another little shake.

Dad smiled a little. "Ah, but—"

Mom held up her hand to stop him. "Besides that, and even more important, you have great faith. Don't give up when things look grim. And I'll be here no matter what."

They were both silent a moment. Then Dad inhaled, as if for the first time in a while, and laughed.

"You're right. I needed a rebuke! I do believe, in fact I *know* that God will bless us for honoring him." He took her hand.

"Ugh, wet," she said.

"Sorry," he said, and scratched his face, leaving foam on an eyebrow. Then he raised his hand, made into a fist, still dripping water. "Now I know how he feels," he said.

"What are you talking about?" Mom asked.

"Misunderstood by the very people who should most appreciate him," Dad said.

"Huh?"

Dad made a rapping motion with his fist. "Knocking on heaven's door."

Mom laughed and rolled her eyes, and their somber mood was broken, so I went back down the hall to my room. I sat and stared at the shadows my hands left on my desk. I tried to form a prayer, but all I could think was, *Please God, don't let my parents quit their music for my sake!*

I heard the phone ring, and Dad answered it. Then I heard both my parents talking. I was thirsty, so I went back down the hall. I heard Dad's full-throated laugh from the kitchen before I stepped in.

"So guess what, Gabe?" Dad said, leaning back against the counter, his ankles crossed.

"I don't know."

"We've been asked to sing at a prestigious conference! Isn't that far out?" he said, and laughed again. "Group hug!" The weight of their arms was comforting.

I sang as I got up and dressed the next morning. It was Saturday, and I planned to go shopping with Carmen. Dad was humming and making toast when I came downstairs.

"Good morning, Gabe!" He grabbed me and messed up my hair.

"Hey," I said, "I just fixed that!"

He released me, and Mom smoothed my hair and kissed my cheek. "Don't mind him, he's a little insane this morning," she said to me in a stage whisper.

"Cruel woman!" Dad said, and plastered butter on his toast. "Okay, so I'm a little excited, I admit. But I'm happy because, on top of that big conference we've been booked for, just this morning a pastor from a local church called and asked us to play at a conference *they're* having today. Their scheduled band canceled." Dad had a wicked look in his eye. "So, one could say that we should give thanks for shoddy behavior, as long as it's not *our* shoddy behavior!"

"Daniel! What a bad example you're setting," Mom said, and patted his cheek.

"Does this mean Carmen and I can't go to the mall?" I asked.

"No, you can still go," Dad said, "but you'll have to walk."

"I don't mind."

"Make sure you take a jacket," Mom said. "It's cold out there."

"Yeah, I know."

I called Carmen to tell her about the change in plans as my parents loaded their equipment in the car. She said her mom could drop her off on her way to do some weekend errands.

My parents were driving away as Carmen and her mother drove up. Carmen ran over to me, her honey-blond hair bouncing with her strides, and I felt as exuberant as she looked. I waved to my parents and then to Carmen's mom as they drove off in different directions.

"Okay, Carmen, all I have to do is grab my stuff and lock the door."

"Hurry up, slowpoke!"

We started off on our walk to the mall, talking and laughing.

There were sirens farther up the street, in our path.

"Someone's in trouble," I said.

"Sounds like it," Carmen said.

We didn't see the car accident until we got closer. There were two ambulances and five police cars at the scene and the distant wail of more approaching emergency vehicles. We joined the crowd at the police barrier and saw two mangled vehicles. I could hear my heartbeat in spite of the commotion and noise. I'd never seen anything so horrible. There were gouges in the pavement where one of the cars had slid upside down for twenty feet. Pieces of glass and metal were scattered over the street like discarded garbage.

"Gabe!" Carmen sounded breathless. "That's your car!"

My blood ran cold as I stared at the twisted wreckage of the car. I pushed people aside and ducked under the yellow police tape.

"Hey, miss!" a cop cried. "You can't come in here!"

I could feel the tape barrier slap my back as I saw two paramedics come out from behind our car with a body on a stretcher. The body was covered with a sheet, except for the left hand, which was hanging down from the side of the stretcher. My eyes were drawn to that hand—it had disciplined me, guided me, and comforted me—my father's hand. He was dead, I knew that. I could see the sparkle of the sun off his ring. I heard, as through a heavy mist, someone yelling.

I woke to a squeezing pressure in my chest and stomach that gave every breath I took a raking pain.

What's wrong with me? I thought. I knew everything had gone black and silent, but I couldn't remember why. I could hear now, but was still surrounded by darkness. My eyes were closed, but I lacked the strength to open them. I heard voices.

"Miss, who is this?"

"My friend, Gabrielle."

Why is Carmen crying?

"What are you doing here? What's wrong with her?"

"We were on our way to the mall and we saw the accident and that's her parents' car," Carmen said.

"You mean the silver one?"

"Yes!"

"*My God!* They, ah, oh *sh*—They didn't make it."

Carmen sobbed louder. "You mean—?"

"They're dead," the voice above said.

I sat up and something struck my head. I was in the back of a police car. Outside the open door, Carmen stood with a hand to her face, crying on an officer's shoulder. With his right hand he patted her back and with his left he rubbed his forehead. His hands were so white I could see large freckles over his skin.

I climbed out of the car and stood. The officer turned to me, his brown eyes sad.

"I'm so sorry," he said, "your parents—Are you all right?"

His hand was on my shoulder, but I couldn't feel it. I managed a slight nod to answer his question. Carmen collapsed against me and sobbed on my shoulder. I could feel the heat of her sobs and hiccups as she clung to me. My arms hung lifeless at my sides.

Chapter
3

$\mathcal{T}$he next thing I remember with any clarity is sitting on the couch in my house, surrounded by people wearing black. I heard whispering.

"The poor child! Can you imagine?"

"She hasn't cried. Or anything."

"What's she going to do?"

I looked down and noticed that my fists had the appearance of carved ice against my black dress. *Those hands must belong to someone else. That would mean it was a mistake that I was in this room listening to these people. A mistake. Yes. Horrible mistake.* I closed my eyes.

"Gabrielle?"

I looked up and recognized Aunt Beatrice. She looked like Mom, though older.

"Honey, how are you doing?" she said, her eyes brimming with tears. "Are you ready to go?"

"Go?" My voice sounded dry and faint.

"To the service."

The pain I'd felt at the sight of Dad on a stretcher throttled me. I tried to bring back the numbness, but I was losing the battle. My eyes hurt. I closed them on darkness and nodded.

At the gravesite I stared at the sprays of flowers draped with a cruel elegance over my parents' coffins.

Why did this happen? I should be with them! There'd be no pain!

I heard Aunt Beatrice beside me, weeping and leaning against tall Uncle Will.

Someone started singing, and a surge of white-hot anger went through me so fast I felt as if my shoes were welded to the ground. *How can you sing!* I thought. *Don't you know that's why they died? They were on the way to sing at that stupid church!*

I wanted to scream at the sky and ask God how he could be so heartless. The violence of my anger frightened me so I had to block it out. The quivering heat faded, and I shook with tremors I couldn't control.

Aunt Beatrice put her arm around me and whispered close to my ear. "It'll be all right, Gabe. I'll take care of you."

I could feel the warmth from her arm and my shaking subsided. *Never. I'll never get that angry again.* I could hear a crackle like ice forming over my heart.

Uncle Will and Aunt Beatrice were Mom's closest relatives and had no children of their own, so my parents named them in their wills as my guardians. Dad's family had disowned him when he became a musician and, even worse in their eyes, a Christian. His father had never spoken to him again. His mother and brothers and sisters had tried to change Dad's mind, but Dad hadn't relented. He could not give up his faith or what he felt he was called to do.

His mom sent flowers to the funeral, but none of his family came.

I was so angry at them I couldn't think straight. I could feel my strength being sucked away in my attempt to fight my anger. *Better never to think of them,* I thought.

Aunt Bea—she insisted I call her that, although it reminded me of reruns of *The Andy Griffith Show*—helped me pack my belongings, and Uncle Will loaded what he could in their car. I saw him packing the rest in boxes, but I didn't care what happened to it. Aunt Bea helped in her fussy way as she could.

She talked to me about their farm while she worked. I tried to hide my horror—I was moving from the urban life of Chicago to a hick, middle-of-nowhere place in North Dakota. I was comfortable in an urban setting. I knew how to get along here. I knew the streets, the corners, the bridges, the dangers. I knew the buildings and the pavement and the debris that would slide past my feet on windy days. And even though every familiar aspect of my life was filled with such pain that breathing was difficult, I dreaded moving into the country. I'd always seen North Dakota through a semihaze of fantasy—part myth, part legend, but not real. I knew Mom grew up there, and I'd been there once, with my parents, when I was five years old. I remembered nothing other than Aunt Bea and Uncle Will from that trip.

And now I had to live in this unknown, hazy Dakota state. I imagined what North Dakota would be like—a frozen, hopeless, flat land populated by weirdos and outcasts. A place where I would be smothered and consumed by loneliness and the outmoded attitudes of old people who had no children.

The trip to Uncle Will and Aunt Bea's place seemed to take a month, though it was only two days. I sat in the back of the car, staring out the window, wondering about school and my friends. *Why should I have to go to a regular public school with a bunch of North Dakota hicks who probably can't read? And what about Carmen?*

She had cried and promised to write at our last meeting. I said nothing.

I stared out at the land shifting past the car. Once we were outside Chicago, I got more nervous about the unknown places and destinations ahead. Uncle Will drove northwest on Interstate 90 into Wisconsin, which joined with Interstate 94 halfway through that state. I already missed the city streets of Chicago as we drove through the woods and hills of Wisconsin. We stopped for the night on the west side of Minneapolis.

The next morning, as we continued westward on Interstate 94, I almost said out loud, *So this is Minnesota. Why would anyone want to live here?* I stared out at the passing scenery—trees and lakes and more trees and lakes. Aunt Bea pointed out some loons on one of the many poolings of water. They were close enough to the road that I could see white speckles on their backs. I stared at their low-slung forms with a kind of yearning, until we were past.

Loons. How appropriate. I wished I could dive underwater like them and escape. *Wasn't there a guy who wrote a book about a trip to a dark jungle? Conrad something. Probably knew what he was talking about. Where are all the people? What is out here anyway?*

The western border of Minnesota brought what I had been dreading—North Dakota. Fargo surprised me. The sprawling, gray city wasn't too bad. I could get used to this.

"Do you live near here?" I asked.

"Oh no, dear," Aunt Bea said. "This is the eastern border of North Dakota. We live near the western border."

Great. How can there be more of nothing? Is there a black hole in the middle of America named North Dakota?

The land beyond Fargo was brown and flat. The only ground I'd seen so flat before was always paved. I could see farms and vehicles that were miles off. The only trees grew in straight rows to separate fields and more fields. I sank back away from the car window. In Minnesota I could not see the ground for the trees and water. Here I could see nothing but ground, and it stretched into infinity. I tried to read a book for a while, but the bare flatness of the land drew my eyes back up.

We stopped in Jamestown for gas and food, and I was relieved to see the town at least had trees and hills. But then we continued west toward Bismarck.

Bismarck. What kind of name is that? How close are we getting to their place? Do I want to get there? I refused to ask again how close we were to where they lived.

The landscape stretched out, hopeless and bare, to the blue horizon miles ahead. Until it changed. It was gradual, so it didn't register at first. We were approaching Bismarck before I realized the change. Now there were hills. I hadn't noticed at first because the hills were like huge waves of water swollen in place. They contained a latent power that surged forward, drawing us farther west. We drove through Bismarck, crossed the Missouri River, then through Mandan, and continued west.

"Did you know that Bismarck is the capital of North Dakota?" Aunt Bea craned around to ask. Nobody was talking much.

"Yeah, sure." I had forgotten. I didn't care.

West of Mandan, the change in landscape became more apparent. The flatness was replaced with rolling grassy hills. I also saw large flat-topped hills at intervals along the horizon. "Oh, look," I said, and pointed to one that was like a picture I had seen of New Mexico. Aunt Bea told me those were called buttes. There were fewer trees now. They were clumped along watercourses and in isolated stands, like sentinels. I noticed cows and horses.

At Dickinson, we got off Interstate 94 and headed north.

"We live near Killdeer," Aunt Bea said.

Is that what they do for fun around here, I thought, *kill deer?*

"The killdeer is a bird," she continued, her voice overlapping my thoughts, "common to North Dakota and one you'll hear often."

A city named after a bird? How original.

"Killdeer is small compared to what you're used to. It's only about eight hundred people, I think."

I was thinking she meant in comparison to pelicans and lake gulls. *But eight hundred! How was that even possible?* Maybe my imagination hadn't been so far off after all.

"We live somewhere between Dickinson and Williston. Williston is nearly fifteen thousand people now."

I could hear the pride in her voice, and I shook my head. *Fifteen thousand? That's a suburb! Why couldn't I stay in Chicago where there were* people?

We were still driving north, but I couldn't look out the window any longer. I closed my eyes to block out the rolling, brownish grasses.

I must have slept, because I heard Aunt Bea say, as if through a tunnel, "Oh thank heaven, we're almost home."

Home. That word echoed in my mind, and I shook my head to clear it. Uncle Will turned the car west again, driving down a gravel road toward the setting sun. The grassy plains surrounding us were gray and lifeless. Then the land dropped away beneath us. I clutched the seat and nearly gasped out loud.

The road wound down through sudden cliffs of brown, tan, red, and yellow—the first color I'd seen in a while. A huge ravine stretched out before us, full of rounded hills and scrubby vegetation. It seemed we'd dropped out of North Dakota and into New Mexico, although there was water here, at the bottom of the ravine. A river or a creek, I didn't know which.

We drove up out of the ravine onto the top of a large hill, still heading west. The road flowed down again, at a gentle slope, the landscape back to rolling grass. I looked out the rear window to make sure I hadn't imagined the ravine. I could only see a glimpse of the far side, and that disappeared as the car moved on.

"That's where we live, honey," Aunt Bea said, pointing to some trees on the right side of the road.

"You live in the trees?"

"You just wait," Uncle Will said, and I could tell he wanted to laugh.

He turned in at their driveway, and I saw that the drive headed toward the southwest corner of a block of trees. There were four rows of trees forming a hollow square. I saw white buildings and corrals, tinged pink-orange by the setting sun, before we pulled up to the house, in the northwest corner of the square. A black dog ran to meet the car.

"That's Oliver," Aunt Bea said, "He was abandoned, so we adopted him. I think he's part coonhound. Will named him after *Oliver Twist*. The neighbor feeds him when we're away."

I got out of the car, stood, and stretched my legs. Oliver trotted over and sniffed me. I held out my hand and he licked it before running back to Uncle Will.

It was darker inside the house than it was outside, until Aunt Bea turned on the lights.

"It is always good to get home," she said.

I stood inside the front door and looked around. I was in a living room, looking into the dining room. There was a staircase and a room to the left, and more rooms to the right. I figured that one of those on the right must be the kitchen, because Aunt Bea had disappeared into it and I could hear her opening and closing cupboard doors.

She stuck her head around the corner. "There you are!" she said. "I'm sorry, I should show you around."

"That's okay."

"Are you hungry?"

I shook my head.

"Well, I'm making tea and toast. Will?"

He came out of a room on the left. Their bedroom, I assumed. "Yes?"

"Would you show Gabe her room?"

"Of course. Yes, I will." The skin at the corners of his blue eyes crinkled, his smile half-hidden by a shaggy mustache. "Here," he said. "Let me take that bag."

I handed it to him and he placed his free arm over my shoulders as we went upstairs. I could feel the strength in the hand resting on my shoulder.

The room he showed me to was on the north side of the house, as he explained, and connected to a bathroom.

"If there's anything you need, just let us know."

"Okay," I said.

He set my bag down and squeezed my shoulder. "Anything, okay?"

I nodded, and he closed the door as he left.

I sat on the bed and stared out a window into the now-dark sky until the window seemed to move toward me. My eyes started to burn. That these were people who knew my parents brought up a sudden burst of tears. I looked down and saw them scattering over my shirt, feeling nothing. I brushed them away and don't know how long I sat there before I went downstairs to the kitchen. Uncle Will was sitting at the table with a cup of tea and Aunt Bea was slicing bread.

"Is your room all right?" she asked.

"Yes, it's nice," I said. I had only really seen the window.

"Have a seat, dear."

I sat down at the table and stared at the steam rising in curls from the cup Aunt Bea placed in front of me. Fear rose through me like suffocating black water—maybe they knew my parents, *but I don't know these people!* I was cold and afraid and I stood up.

"I know it's kind of early," I said, "but I think I'll go to bed, if that's okay."

"Of course it's okay!" Aunt Bea said. "Traveling can be so tiring. Besides, it's an hour later for you."

"What?"

"We're in a different time zone now. Chicago is on Central time. We're on Mountain time. Only an hour earlier, but it will probably take you a while to adjust."

"Oh." I stepped away from the table. "Well, uh, goodnight then," I said, and walked out of the kitchen. I stopped at the top of the stairs because I could hear them talking.

"The poor child," Aunt Bea said. "It breaks my heart to see her suffer so."

"Give her time, Bea. Don't push her."

I went into what was now supposed to be my room, closed the door and leaned against it, trembling.

Time for what? To pretend nothing has happened? To pretend I'm happy? What do they know anyway?

I realized I was tired, even though saying so had been a way to get away from them. I crawled into bed fully clothed.

I woke to a night so black I felt blind. I was used to an orange glow of streetlights, but there was nothing here to block the full darkness of night. I heard the wind moaning through the trees outside the house. It was the loneliest sound I could imagine at this point in my life. An iron hand was squeezing my chest and suffocating me, my body damp with a cold sweat. I sat up and grabbed my knees, trying to push air out of my chest. I forced myself to breathe until the pain faded. I felt cold inside and out. I lay back down and listened to the mourning wind.

Chapter
4

The next morning, after breakfast, Uncle Will offered to show me more of their ranch. We stepped out into a clear, cool morning.

Uncle Will sucked a long breath through his nose. "The air smells better here than anywhere else I've been."

I inhaled. I had never noticed the smell of clean air before. I couldn't even think of how to describe it, but there was a crispness that made my nose tingle.

"It's nice," I said, the first pleasant thing I meant since our trip began.

I was getting over my fear of Uncle Will. He was quiet, and that initially made me uncomfortable because I thought he didn't want me around. I came to realize that he was, by nature, a quiet person. Perhaps that is why he and Aunt Bea got along so well—Aunt Bea liked to talk and Uncle Will was content to listen. I felt more at ease with him than Aunt Bea once I understood that. I felt he sensed my feelings without either of us needing to speak. Or maybe I preferred his company because he didn't require talking. Speaking was painful for me, so Aunt Bea's chattiness often grated. I was grateful that she didn't seem to expect a response.

I looked around at the yard in the morning light and saw an arena inside the large oval formed by the drive. In the southeast corner of the yard was a large barn with corrals attached and, on the south side, near where the drive entered the yard, a smaller barn.

Uncle Will talked as we walked toward the larger barn. "We

raise cows and horses here. The cows we sell. The horses, well, I get attached to them so they're harder to sell. The cows are out in pasture. So are most of the horses, but they come up to the barn for water."

I noticed a big double C formed out of boards on the main barn doors. Uncle Will slid back one of the doors, explaining that the ranch was the Chamberlain Crescent Ranch, therefore the brand was CC.

"My grandfather bought the ranch and registered the brand," Uncle Will said. "It's never been changed. When I inherited the place, the only change I made was to buy some land and build up the ranch more."

The inside of the barn was striped with streams of light filtering through windows with clouded panes. Dust motes sailed in storms across the rays of light. I could almost feel them settling in the silence. The barn was quiet, full of pungent odors I couldn't identify. The light streaming through the windows deepened the shadows in the rest of the barn, and the shadows created a sense of waiting. But the streams of light created a pleasant, welcoming sense.

"This is nice," I said, my voice muted by the size of the barn.

"My grandfather and his neighbors built it when my father was a boy. I've always been able to think in here."

I looked at Uncle Will to see if he was joking, but he stood, quiet, as if stilled for a thought before speaking. "Here, let me show you something."

I followed him to a stall at the side of the barn. A horse stuck its head over the door and nickered.

"Have you had much experience with horses?" Uncle Will looked down at me. The blue of his eyes was pale and intense, yet the expression was calm.

"I took a few riding lessons. I've always liked horses."

"Well, the first thing to know is that horses are very good at reading feelings, so don't act timid, but don't move too quickly."

I nodded and watched as he stroked the horse's forehead. "This is Belle, one of my broodmares. You can pet her."

I stroked her nose, surprised to find it soft as silk. Her nostrils fluttered with her breath and her red forelock fell over her eyes as she dropped her nose into my hand. I heard rustling and a squeal. Belle swung her head back and nickered. A colt levered himself out of the straw with ridiculously-long-looking legs, and started nursing.

Uncle Will went into the stall. "Come on in," he said.

I followed him in, avoiding the manure. The colt came up to us, drops of milk decorating his whiskers like wet pearls. His eyelashes stuck straight out from his head, making his eyes look rounder than they were. He nibbled on my jacket, and I ran my hand over his mane, which stood up in a Mohawk. His coat was deep red, mahogany, and as soft as new flannel. I was amazed at how perfect his legs and hooves were, even though they were so small.

Uncle Will stepped over to the other side of the stall, to another door. "I'm going to let them out," he said.

The door opened into an adjoining corral, and I watched the colt run and kick up his heels. It occurred to me how much my parents would love this, and a jolt of anger, guilt, and loneliness twisted through me in a tight braid. I turned and stared at the inside of the barn, commanding myself to calm down.

Uncle Will came in and closed the stall door. We walked down the barn, and he showed me other mares that were due to foal.

We left the big barn and walked toward the smaller one, passing a round corral with a six-foot-high fence, the wooden boards close together.

"What's that for?" I asked.

"That's a round pen," Uncle Will said. "It's for training horses.

See, the first few times you ride a horse, it helps to be in a corral you know they can't get out of. That way, you don't have to worry about them running away. Maybe just about them bucking. I'll show you someday." He smiled. "Well, I hope not the bucking part."

We entered the smaller barn and heard a loud whinny from a horse leaning as far out of its stall as possible, tossing its head.

"Hey, old man, how's it going?" Uncle Will asked, and slapped the horse's neck. "This is my top stud. We call him General because he thinks he can order everyone around."

General was a beautiful silver-gray horse with a long, dark-gray mane and tail. Uncle Will turned him out also, and I watched him run around his corral. He would run with his head held high, then drop his head, writhing his neck like a snake. After a last buck, he dropped to the ground and rolled.

I heard Oliver bark and the sound of a pickup driving up.

"That must be our neighbor, Jim," Uncle Will said, and we left the barn. I saw Oliver leaping around an old, dented pickup as the neighbor stepped out. The door creaked as he slammed it.

"Thanks for watching the place while we were away, Jim," Uncle Will said, and shook his hand.

"That's what neighbors are for," Jim said. "And it was the least I could do."

"Jim, this is my niece, Gabrielle Larson."

"Glad to make your acquaintance, young lady," Jim said, and extended his hand. It was dry and chapped, and his hair was rumpled.

"I think I'll go back to the house," I said.

"Okay," Uncle Will said.

"Nice to meet you," Jim said as I walked away. Oliver trotted by my side, glancing up at me, tongue sliding sideways out of his open mouth. I bent to pet him before entering the house and was rewarded with a lick on the cheek.

I heard Aunt Bea playing the piano and singing when I entered the house. Anger spread through me. I moved closer on shaking legs. I felt as if my blood had drained to my feet. The heaviness of both feet held me in place behind Aunt Bea. She turned on the piano bench and smiled at me with tears in her eyes.

"Your mother and I used to sing together all the time. Gabe, are you all right? You're pale."

My face was so cold it felt frozen, immobile.

"I *hate* music!" I said. "It killed my parents, and I never want to hear it again!"

I ran upstairs, leaving Aunt Bea sitting at the piano with her mouth open. I dropped onto my bed and pulled my knees up to my chest. I heard a soft knock on my door.

"Gabrielle? May I please come in?" Aunt Bea asked.

I was shaking so hard I couldn't answer. I heard her open the door.

"Gabrielle, I am so sorry, I didn't think. You poor child!" She knelt down and hugged me. There was a faint, pungent smell about her, not entirely pleasant.

"Please forgive me, Gabe, I didn't think how much that would hurt you. I'm so sorry, will you please forgive me?"

I managed to nod, and she stroked my hair until I stopped shaking.

"Feel better now?"

I sat up, but avoided looking at her. "Sorry I reacted like that," I said, my lips having trouble forming the words.

"No, no, it's okay, honey, it was my fault. Do you want to help me with lunch?"

I nodded.

"Okay then. Let's go downstairs. No more talk about it."

Aunt Bea soon found work for me in the kitchen. The ringing phone interrupted our work, and Aunt Bea picked it up.

PAST DARKNESS

"Hello? Oh, hi Emily! How have things been going? Do I have lots of appointments? Uh-huh. Right, I see. Well, I'll be in tomorrow. All right, see you then. Bye, honey." She hung up the phone. "Well, it looks like it's back to the daily grind." She smiled at me. "You know I'm a veterinarian?"

"Yes." I had forgotten, but that could explain her antibacterial smell.

"If you want," she said, "you could come to the office with me tomorrow and check things out."

"Yeah, sure. I like animals."

I went with Aunt Bea to her clinic in Watford City the next day. I was surprised by two things—that it took about forty minutes to get there, and by their use of "city," since its population was under two thousand.

We pulled up to a steel building with chutes and corrals in the back, and I saw a sign that read: *Beatrice Chamberlain, DVM*, which matched the logo on Aunt Bea's pickup doors.

"Well, this is it." I could detect a note of pride in her voice. "Come in and see what it's all about."

The front door opened on a waiting area with a desk. A young woman sitting behind it rose as we entered.

"Good morning, Bea," she said, and smiled. "It's good to have you back."

"It's good to be back! Gabe, this is Emily, my assistant. Emily, Gabe."

Emily came forward and extended her hand. She was tall and thin, and the short blond hair falling in ringlets around her ears gave her a groomed, feline look.

"It's nice to meet you," she said, and we shook hands. Hers was hard as Uncle Will's, her voice soft and raspy.

"Nice to meet you, too," I said. She smiled at me, but her green eyes were as cool as Lake Michigan in springmelt.

There was a hallway off the waiting area, and down it, on each side, were several doors. At the far end of the room was a heavier door, and I could hear noises from the other side.

"Mr. Johnson's in the back with his prize bull," Emily said.

"Okay," Aunt Bea said, "I better see him right away. Want to come, Gabe?"

I nodded, not comfortable staying with Emily. We went through the heavy door into the back part of the building, which had corrals and chutes leading into it. A man dressed in Wranglers, denim jacket, and—my goodness!—a cowboy hat, was leaning against one of the corrals and talking to his bull, a big black beast whose gentle, confused eyes were contradicted by his thick-muscled neck and forequarters.

"Good morning, Bruce," Aunt Bea said. "So Angus is giving you trouble again?"

"You know Angus," Bruce said, "not happy unless he's in trouble."

"So, what's he done this time?"

"He musta got caught in a fence. See, he tore his leg up real good." Bruce pointed to the bull's right front leg.

"So I see." Aunt Bea bent down to look closer. "The good news for Angus is it's mostly superficial. Could you get him in the squeeze chute while I gather my instruments?"

Mr. Johnson nodded and walked around to the other side of the corral and opened the chute while I stared at the bull's leg. It looked horrible to me. There were several long gashes below the knee, and thick blood kept dripping down into the bull's fur and unto his hoof. The blood had mixed with dirt to form a gummy paste on the bull's hoof.

Mr. Johnson got Angus in the chute, and Aunt Bea cleaned and stitched his leg. Once she had finished, I could see why she had said it was a superficial wound. Angus's leg now had two rows of neat stitches that hardly showed against his dark skin.

"That should do it. I can give him a tetanus shot also."

"Better do that. Never know what he'll do next."

We went back inside, saw several people in the waiting area, and then went down the hallway to an exam room for smaller animals. Emily brought the first client back—an older lady with a fat, coughing poodle in tow. My fascination with sick and injured animals grew as the day progressed.

Aunt Bea began talking on our way back to the ranch. "I always knew I wanted to be a vet," she said. "I left the state to go to school, but I felt pulled back to North Dakota. I can't explain it, but I felt drawn to a small-town practice. In a sense there is more variety because you have the ranchers with their horses and cattle, the town-folk with their pets, and everybody in between. I worked with the vet in Watford City for a while after I was licensed, until he retired. Then I took over. Before that, though, I met your Uncle Will. In a sense, it seemed like that was why I moved back here, to find your uncle!"

I stared out at the grassy hills. *Yeah, right,* I thought.

"Will was different from most young men from around here. He was kinder and quieter, yet when he said something there was a weight behind it, as if he'd thought about what he was going to say. And then when he smiled or laughed! Oh my, what a handsome guy!" Aunt Bea laughed, a merry, trilling sound. I smiled in spite of my skepticism.

I spent time outside every day, and I finally realized that seasonal changes were different outside the city. I thought it was supposed to be spring here, but it often didn't feel like spring. There was an ethereal, temperate feel to the air, yet winter seemed to be hanging above, waiting with frosty teeth. The sun got warmer and closer over time, and though the wind often had an icy edge, I began to feel the sun's strength. It had to win, I knew.

I went to work with Aunt Bea a couple of times a week and always enjoyed the experience. I also helped Uncle Will with his ranch work. It didn't always go well, especially the first time I attempted to help him work some horses.

It was a clear day, but breezy, and Uncle Will commented on it as we walked toward the barn. "I hope the wind doesn't pick up more," he said. "It makes horses a little edgy, especially the young ones."

"Why?" I asked, matching my walk to his long stride.

"Horses can smell new scents in the wind. And it's in a horse's nature to be suspicious of things they can smell and hear but not see. It's a survival instinct, see, from the days when wild horses feared everything unknown. Also, things tend to flap around and make funny noises when it's windy. Horses'll shy or spook."

Uncle Will explained that he wanted to sort his yearlings by separating the fillies from the colts. Once this was done, he would be able to put the colts in with some of his studs and geldings and the fillies out with his mares. He would also be able to better judge which ones he wanted to keep and which he would sell.

We stopped beside one of the large corrals. It was full of young horses, some stretched out in the sun, others chewing on the backs of their neighbors in a nonchalant manner.

"Gabrielle, you know you have to be careful around horses, right?" He waited for me to nod before continuing. "If you move too quickly, you can spook them, but if you're too tentative they might ignore you and run into you. The main thing is, while you're learning, when I tell you to do something, you do it as fast as you can and as well as you can. Understand?"

I nodded, but he must have sensed my apprehension.

"Horses can also sense fear, so be as calm as possible." He smiled down at me and added, "I'm not trying to scare you, Gabrielle. I want to make sure you understand there are risks in everything you do out here—I'm trying to tell you how to keep yourself as safe as possible."

My response was a tentative smile.

"Now, what I want you to do is stand at this gate here and open it when I have a filly sorted out so she can run into this other pen. Just stand here with the gate closed, and I'll tell you when to open it. Simple, right?"

"Right," I said.

"Okay!"

Uncle Will went through the gate, dragging the end of a long whip behind him. He'd explained to me, when he saw me looking at it, that the whip was only to remind the frisky yearlings that he meant business.

"The only time I strike them is if they try to strike me first!" he said, and winked.

I stood at the gate, the wind tangling loose strands of my hair while the metal of the gate grew colder under my fingers. The warmth was fading fast as clouds covered the sky from horizon to horizon. I watched Uncle Will move among the yearlings, cutting out one filly after another, and sending them in my direction. He'd call out, "Gate!" and I'd swing it open and watch the filly go through. Some walked, some pranced, some snorted and hesitated, some trotted or leaped.

Uncle Will was having problems with a lanky gray filly. She kept ducking away from him and pushing into a group of yearlings or dodging into a corner and dropping her head and refusing to move. I heard Uncle Will muttering at her as he walked across the corral after her once again, but he stayed calm. Then she rushed by him, nearly running into him.

"Stupid knot-head!" he yelled, and I turned away. I didn't want to see his anger. I focused on the ground and feeling my hair blowing against my cold cheeks. I heard Uncle Will say something indistinctly, then he yelled, "GATE!" I looked up to see the gray filly loping at me, so I jerked the gate open. I moved too fast. Another little filly had wandered up behind me, curious, and the swinging gate hit her side. She spooked and jumped sideways into the corral fence. The gray filly snorted and shied from the gate, returning to the other yearlings. Uncle Will, his face red and sweaty, lashed the ground with his whip.

"Good grief! Didn't your parents teach you any sense?"

The silence that followed those words crackled like an electric line gone bad. I held my breath. Uncle Will stared at me, then lowered his head, raising a hand to his forehead. I didn't move. I watched the little filly step back toward the other horses, shaking, not so curious anymore.

My knuckles went white as my grip on the gate tightened, the metal so cold it was burning my hand. Uncle Will shifted his weight to one hip and dropped his hand to his lower back. Then he looked at me. I watched him walk toward me, my body tense and cold. He came through the gate, pulled it from my grip, and swung it closed. My hand fell to my side, my fingers still holding the shape of the metal bar. Uncle Will stood looking over the gate, not facing me.

"Gabrielle. That was a terrible thing for me to say." I could hear sorrow in his voice. "I never should have said it, and I certainly didn't mean it. Nothing can take the words back, but please understand that I didn't want to hurt you." He turned to me. "I should have let them settle before going after that ornery filly. Can you forgive me?"

He reached out and took my hand in his warm, sweaty one. "Your hand's like ice!" The concern in his voice forced me to look up. His eyes looked full of the same warmth. He rubbed my hand between his. I closed my eyes and bit my lip.

I opened my eyes and looked at him. "I know you didn't mean it," I said. "I wanted to help, and now I've hurt one."

"She's fine," he said. "In fact, maybe she learned to look before she leaps!" He smiled and put his arm over my shoulders and pulled me toward the yearlings. I could feel warmth from him as he sheltered me from the wind. The little filly turned toward us and pricked her ears.

"Here, pretty little one," Uncle Will said. She took a few steps in our direction. We walked up to her, and she looked at us with curiosity.

"Go ahead, pet her," Uncle Will said.

I ran my hand down her smooth neck.

"See, she's just fine. A sweet little girl." She tried to nibble his sleeve as he rubbed her forehead. "Ah, now. None of that," he said, and covered her mouth with his other hand.

"Let's take our long-overdue break, shall we?"

Aunt Bea looked up from some papers she had spread across the kitchen table.

"How'd it go? You're pale, Gabe! Is anything wrong?"

"No, Bea, nothing at all," Uncle Will said. "We decided to take a break. It's a little colder out there than it looks."

I was so grateful to him for not explaining, I collapsed on a nearby chair.

"Why Will, I think you tired her out! Are you tired, Gabe?"

"A little."

Chapter
5

We settled into a pattern together. I learned something every day from working with Uncle Will, and at the clinic from Aunt Bea. She said I was good with animals, had what she called a calming touch, and added that it was a trait that ran through women in the family. She remembered how her grandmother calmed animals by laying a hand on them and whispering close in Norwegian.

I started school again at the end of my first month in North Dakota, even though there was only a month left in the school year. I soon caught up in class work—I had always done well in school—but didn't make any friends. I felt older than my classmates and, though they were friendly, I maintained a polite distance. I was relieved when the school year ended.

I went to the clinic with Aunt Bea during the summer. I also tried to copy Uncle Will's patience as he began training young horses. We enjoyed relaxing rides through the grassy hills on their ranch, checking cattle and fence lines.

On these rides we would stop on a hilltop to look out over the land. The breeze would force the knee-high grass into bowing waves that would rush up the hill toward us, swirling in eddying patterns I'd seen only in water. There was either a small river or a creek that ran through all of Uncle Will's pastureland. These waterways were visible from most hilltops because they were lined with trees or had clumps of shrubs along one bank or another. I'd never seen so few trees, but I'd also never appreciated trees until I lived where they were a scarce commodity.

It's true what they say, I thought. *You can't see the forest for the trees.*

Sitting on a horse—surrounded by moving grass, watching clouds grow in the brilliant sky that stretched out to anchor us to the buttes standing in stacks on the distant horizon—opened something in me. I observed the land and weather in a way I hadn't before. In Chicago the weather was hot in the summer, windy and rainy in the spring and fall, and windy and cold in the winter. Here, one day could be as different as the next. The summer days could be hot, still, and even humid. Then the next day would be windy and cool. I loved the unpredictability.

I loved those moments when we would sit and listen. The breeze carried to us the cries of eagles and hawks, the twitter of songbirds, the distant whinnies of horses and lowing of cattle, and the smells of grass, of water lined by reedy mud, and of sweet air purified by distant pinewoods—as near as the Badlands and as far west as the mountains of Montana and Wyoming, perhaps.

I had been at the ranch for almost four months when one of the year's most important events arrived—branding time. All the cattle had to be rounded up so the calves could be branded. Since it was a necessary event, Aunt Bea took a few days off work so she could help. Uncle Will had already told me that it was an unspoken policy between him and the other ranchers in the area that they helped one another at branding time.

The day of the roundup, we got up before sunrise and saddled the horses we'd shut in the barn overnight. By the time the sun rose, the yard was full of the trucks, trailers, and horses of the neighbors. I was scrutinized by the children of the other ranchers as they showed off for one another, warming up their horses in Uncle Will's arena.

Uncle Will came up to me as I was putting the bridle on the horse I would be riding.

"Gabrielle," he said, "you should stay close to me today. Okay?"

"Okay," I said. That was fine with me. I wouldn't feel so lost.

Uncle Will explained to everyone which pasture we were going to gather the cow-calf pairs out of and where we were driving them. The riders spread out across the pasture, sweeping the cattle in the right direction. I stayed close to Uncle Will. We checked the ravines, pushing out any stray cows and calves. Soon the grass was darkened by the herd of cows trailing away toward the corrals.

The landscape around me opened up as we were riding along. I stopped, certain I would hear the land speak if I stayed still enough. My horse remained motionless too, sensing my expectation. I looked around, hardly breathing. The green of the knee-high grass, lighter in color at the heads, rippled into different colors to speed along the ground as the wind traveled through it. On the hillsides, mixed with the grass, were silvery gray-green tufts of sage that released a pungent aroma when it was crushed by hooves. Farther away, along the banks of a creek, I could see the dark, reedy green of water grass. Even farther away were the misty features of distant buttes—the purple-green haze that faded into the bright blue of the summer sky, scoured clean by wind and sun. I was surrounded by space, and I realized that I had grown to love it more than the city streets that had faded from my consciousness, like a bad dream in the tangible light of day.

I welcomed the emptiness of the open space. It was cleaner than anything I'd seen, and it was out of this clarity that I expected to hear something. I looked around, waiting.

I could see the predator birds gliding high in the hard sky, the flit of songbirds, the graceful movements of waterbirds. I could hear the keening *cra-cra-cra-baba* or *kill-deer, kill-deer* of the long-legged killdeer and the grating honks of the otherwise graceful mallard ducks. And the birds I had at first mistaken for owls—the mourning doves—sang a prayerful *who-who-whooo*, which I heard most often as the sun sank, reddening the western side of everything it touched. The mourning doves seemed to herald the later sounds of the coyotes. Their staccato yips and undulating, mournful howls filled clear starry nights, sounding joyful, maddened, crazed, and full of a dreadful sadness all at once. I could tolerate that.

A shrill whistle snapped me out of my reverie. I saw Uncle Will driving some cattle out of a ravine. My horse shook its head, snorted, and jerked at the bit.

"Okay, let's go," I said.

My horse sprang into a trot, heading toward Uncle Will, the instinct to herd bred into him. The hill in front of us was now covered with cattle, reluctant to plod up. They wanted to take the easier route, back down the hill the way they'd come. We urged them over the hill and into the pen below, so we could sort out the calves to be branded.

I'd never seen anything like it, and it took a while to get used to the hectic scene. One of the riders would rope a calf and pull it out of the herd so a person on the ground could hold a branding iron against its hip. I flinched the first few times I saw it, but the calves were more concerned with being separated from their mothers. Once freed, they trotted back to the herd to find their mothers, shaking their heads, a CC now visible in their soft fur. I wasn't of much use during the branding. I watched as boys younger than I roped calves like experts, working their horses deep into the herd and emerging with a calf in tow. About all I did was fetch for Uncle Will.

I welcomed our lunch break that day. My legs were sore, since I hadn't ridden so much at one time before. Aunt Bea drove a pickup full of sandwiches and drinks out to the branding site, and we all rested for a while after eating. Most of the boys were on the ground practicing their roping. I went over to tie my horse in the shade of a tree so it could graze for a while. One of the older boys, my age probably, walked over close to me to move his horse as well. He had a distinct walk, not a swagger really, but close to it. I recognized him from school. I never saw him out of jeans and boots, unless he was required to wear something else.

He came over to me after tying his horse.

"Hey," he said, "my name's Duncan. You're Gabrielle, right?"

His directness was unexpected, but not unpleasant.

"Yes."

"This your first roundup?" he asked.

"Yes."

"I've been doing them since I could ride."

He uncoiled the lariat he'd been carrying over his shoulder and began shaking out the loops. His arms were brown, his face in shadow because his hat was pulled so low. The silence became awkward to me, but Duncan didn't seem to mind. He kept adjusting his rope and tossing it over a clump of sage nearby.

"Uh," I said, "that's a pretty horse you're riding."

"Ain't she, though?" Duncan said. "I trained her myself." I could hear the pride in his voice as he studied her. "My dad doesn't like mares, not for riding anyway. He says they're too nervous. So I said, 'Shoot, Dad, you can ride the geldings, I'll ride the mares!' And you saw the knot-head he was riding today. Geez, he needs to sell that hammer-headed nag."

Duncan laughed and shook his head. "My little mare can run circles around that gelding, but Dad won't admit it. He learned from his daddy that mares were no good." Duncan shrugged and tossed his rope again, a perfect throw. "It makes no difference to me if I ride a mare, gelding, or stud. Just so long as it's a good horse! Mr.

Chamberlain, now, he's got some great horses. Might have to buy me some one day." He smiled at me.

"I like Uncle Will's horses, too," I said.

"Your uncle, he runs a good operation. And you did good today, kid."

"Thanks."

"Aw, shoot. I better go hog-tie my brother before he starts a stampede."

Duncan walked toward his brother, who was chasing one of the other boys, swinging his rope and whooping. Duncan joined in the tussle and managed to get the other boys to settle down. I watched as he showed them how to improve their roping technique. They seemed to be having fun. I turned away and saw all the grown-ups gathered around one of the pickups, gesturing in speech I couldn't hear. I turned back to my horse, petting his smooth neck as he tore up the grass and chewed in contentment.

It was amazing to see all these people working together, helping each other. I'd never experienced a community of this sort. I was accepted as Will Chamberlain's niece, it seemed, but I still felt out of place.

Chapter
6

I was on the ranch by myself for the first time on a hot day in late summer. Aunt Bea was at work and Uncle Will had driven to Williston to get a part for his baler. He told me not to do anything with the horses because of the heat. I decided to stay inside and read.

I walked out to check the mail just after noon and noticed clouds building up in the southwest. They looked far away. I was reading *Jane Eyre*, caught up in Jane's dilemma of whether to leave Mr. Rochester. Not long after I'd started reading again, I noticed that the house was dark, even though it was early afternoon. I looked up from my book and saw only darkness out the windows to the west and south.

I walked through the house, looking out different windows, getting more concerned by the minute. *What should I do?* I thought. *I've never seen clouds like that!*

I made sure all the windows were shut. Then I remembered the barn.

I ran across the yard, through still air, the heat pressing down in ominous silence. I stepped inside the barn, gasping. Ollie sat next to me and whined, his tongue flicking over his nose, in and out, several times.

The smaller doors were closed, so I stepped outside to slide the main doors shut since they had to be latched from the outside. The temperature dropped fast. It looked like the weirdly-green clouds were brushing the treetops.

A cold wind swept through the trees with a low-pitched whistle, bending their tops, and I ran back to the house. Ollie ran ahead of me, tail down. I heard the first crack and grumble of lightning and thunder. I crashed through the back door, shaking, and Ollie followed me in. I let him stay in the kitchen.

The house was dark. I turned on a few lights and walked through the downstairs. The rumbles of thunder outside grew louder. I checked the clouds on all sides of the house. My legs trembled, and I couldn't stand still. The flashes of lightning made the night-dark yard shine neon green for a few seconds. The gnashing eruptions of thunder seemed to grow out of the darkness that followed each flash of lightning.

Black clouds overlapped livid gray clouds, the lower ones moving more quickly. The wind stirred the tops of the trees in circular waves—the yard felt hushed in expectation. I was the one not expecting this.

The yard flashed bright as day for a moment, as lightning struck so close I heard the sizzle of the bolt, followed by a crushing clap of thunder so loud my ears rang and the windows shook. I screamed and ran into the kitchen. Ollie jumped up and barked. The house was black, lit only by the intermittent flashes of electric-looking light.

I found a flashlight and went into the basement. I sat on the floor, shivering, burying the fingers of one hand in Oliver's fur, snapping the flashlight on and off with the other. Patches of light flashed on the floor through narrow windows above as the lightning continued unabated. The wind and thunder was so loud I felt buried alive, with reality muffled. *What if this is a tornado?* I thought. *If it is, how will I hear it through the noise?*

Ollie shifted closer and sighed, leaning his head on my leg. I rubbed his head and felt his soft tongue on my fingers. I flicked the flashlight on again. Ollie rolled his eyes at me and slapped his tail once on the floor. The lightning flashes continued, jarring my nerves with their uneven, unending strobe-light florescence.

Rain beat against the house like waves of surf. I thought the worst of the storm had broken, so I resumed my pacing upstairs. Through the flashes of lightning, I could see the rain coming down in nearly horizontal waves. The water ran unbroken down the west and south windows. Through the east and north windows I could see the trees bent forward by the wind and rain, whipping upright, only to be bent forward again.

I made several rounds of the house before realizing Ollie was following me. I went and sat in the kitchen and made him lie on the floor. I watched water wash down the kitchen windows, as if someone were pouring buckets of it off the roof. *Or like I'm in a giant car wash.*

The storm felt hours long, but the rain lessened, the lightning faded, and the clouds parted. I realized it was only midafternoon when the sun came through the clouds. I stepped outside. The sun sparkled off the raindrops hanging on leaves and grass. I was in a washed, golden-green world. The puddles in the driveway reflected the receding clouds and the growing expanse of blue.

I went inside to call Aunt Bea to see if the storm had hit there. The phone was dead. The power was out. I was alone.

I heard Uncle Will's pickup in the yard and went outside. Seeing him step out of his pickup sent a feeling of security through me.

"Was the storm bad here?" Uncle Will asked.

"Yeah. The power's out. So is the phone."

I felt detached from the experience now that it was over. It had the feeling of an event from a different past.

Uncle Will whistled. "It sure did rain, didn't it?"

I nodded.

"I was driving through what must have been the tail-end of

the storm, and my wipers couldn't keep up with the rain. I had to pull over until I could see to drive. For a minute, I thought I'd be washed away!"

"It was raining so hard I couldn't even see raindrops on the windows, just a solid sheet of water."

"That's some rain!" Uncle Will looked around the yard. "And you closed the barn. Good job! It will be nice and dry."

He rested his hand on my shoulder and everything settled in fine.

As the hot summer lengthened toward fall, I discovered that one of the hardest jobs I'd ever had was also one of the most rewarding—making hay. Uncle Will used small square bales to feed to his horses. He also rolled up huge round bales to feed his cattle.

Uncle Will pulled a hayrack behind his square baler, so someone else had to ride on the hayrack while he was baling, to stack the bales as they emerged from the tail end of the baler. This became my job. At first, unused to the work, I could only lift the bales with a struggle, and I was soon hot, dusty, and tired. Uncle Will must have realized this because he took frequent breaks. I don't know if he knew my pride would be hurt if he suggested I couldn't do the job, or if he thought it would be good for me to toughen up, but I was glad he let me struggle on. It was hard but rewarding to see the neat stacks of bales growing larger.

I settled into a rhythm as I rode behind the baler—stacking the fresh-packed bales—following the tempo set by the metallic *ka-chung* of the baler packing the hay. The fine dust from the hay clung to my damp skin, stinging in the minute scratches on my arms caused by the sharp-cut ends of grass and stems on each bale's sides. I was surrounded by the healthy smell of grass and sage.

Alfalfa hay was heavier and even dustier than prairie hay. The green leaves powdered into an itchy dust that settled over everything, smelling like sweet tea. Prairie hay was my favorite to work with. The scent became to me the quintessential smell of summer— grass dried by sun and wind, mixed with sage and clumps of wild clover and alfalfa. Even in the middle of winter, when I would break open a bale of grass hay, the smell of summer rose in shimmering heat waves toward my face, coating my skin with the remembered dust and sweat of haying.

I felt I'd progressed as a ranch hand when Uncle Will let me rake hay by myself. He needed to repair the baler, so he showed me how to operate the rake and then left me to rake the hay into windrows while he worked on the baler.

I was raking a second cutting of hay in a small field of alfalfa. The weather had dried out after the rains of spring and early summer, so this second cutting was sparse.

I was using a small tractor with no cab, so I was exposed to the dust kicked up by the rake's toothed wheels. The wheels spun the cut alfalfa into neat windrows, and the teeth on the wheels raised dust as they scraped the ground.

I was hot and sweaty when I returned to the house. Aunt Bea laughed at me.

"What's so funny?" I said.

"Look in a mirror, honey!"

I went upstairs to change my clothes. I realized, when I looked in a mirror, that it wasn't just my clothes that were dusty. My hair and face were powdered with it.

I smiled, teeth looking pure white, and could hardly believe the amount of dark water as I washed my hands. Its clear run turned black from the dirt on my face and was sucked away in a whirl of water.

So the summer went, and so school began again. I still felt like an outsider. Most of my classmates had known each other all their lives. I knew I was to blame for not being well-liked, since the students thought I was stuck-up because I didn't join their games and conversations or try to feign friendliness. I was polite, but that only seemed to annoy them. A few disliked me in a larger sense because I was good in the classes they liked least, such as math and science.

The only one who really talked to me was Duncan, but I didn't see him often. He would pass me in the hall and say, "Hey, kid, how's it going?" And then he would pause and wait for a response, although he always seemed to be in a hurry.

Aunt Bea interrupted me one night when I was doing biology homework.

"Gabrielle," she said, "have you ever considered becoming a veterinarian?"

I looked at her and tapped my pencil on a page of the textbook. "No, I guess not. Why?"

"Well, you are really good in science and you're also good with animals. I just wondered if you'd ever considered becoming a vet or something of the kind."

I set down my pencil.

"I'm not saying this because I'm a vet," Aunt Bea said. "I just think it would be a good option for you to consider. Of course, if you need any information, you know who to ask!" She smiled at me and I smiled back.

"I'll keep it in mind," I said.

"That's all I ask!"

The routine at school continued. I would go out to work with the horses when I got home from school, to block out the hurt of not fitting in with others because I wouldn't bend or change. The horses accepted me. So did Uncle Will. He was a no-fuss-or-nonsense type of guy, and he did the job at hand with the ease of practice and patience. Yet he was artistic in his own way and could see beauty in everyday life. He would pause in the middle of work and marvel at the sheen of the sun on a horse's coat or a hawk suspended in flight. He could pack bales in tight stacks that would shed rain, and plot out new, straight fence lines.

I was most at ease with him. He didn't demand conversation, but rather worked and explained necessary details as we went along—which was unlike Aunt Bea's way of talking everything through. She was a combination of nervous energy and calm. She could deal with an animal's injury as if it were the most normal thing in the world. Yet she needed to be involved in activity all the time. If Uncle Will and I were reading or even watching a movie, Aunt Bea would be busy at some sort of craftwork. She seemed incapable of total rest and calm—when she wasn't able to do something physically, she talked.

I thought it was interesting that although Aunt Bea had gone through double the schooling of Uncle Will, who stopped after high school, he seemed better educated. She was smart about anything scientific and animal-anatomy-related. But he had a keen, analytical mind and an abundance of common sense, along with a literary sharpness that surprised me. While his rancher friends read Zane Grey and Louis L'Amour novels, Uncle Will read William Faulkner and Leo Tolstoy. I picked up and read every book that he read after he finished it. I was amazed at the beauty I found in stories such as *Anna Karenina* or Willa Cather's *O! Pioneers!* Inside the flyleaf of one of those well-worn books I saw, in small, neat cursive, *Margaret Smith*. I never asked Uncle Will who she was.

Chapter
7

I had been on the Crescent Ranch for over a year before I realized some of the reasons for Uncle Will's contemplative nature. We were checking fence lines on horseback on a mild, breezy day, and stopped on the crest of a ravine to look at the landscape.

Uncle Will pointed. "See where that creek enters the ravine up ahead?" he asked.

"Yes."

"That was the original property line to the west, when my grandfather ran the ranch. I added the land farther west later."

"Uncle Will," I said, "how come you never talk about your father?"

He lowered his hands to the saddle horn, crossing them over each other, as though in prayer. He stared straight ahead, squinting at the western horizon.

"I don't remember much good about my father and this place," he said. "I was twelve when he left here the last time. He and Grandpa got along like two raccoons in a gunnysack, so he left when he finished high school, and moved from city to city. That's how he met my mother, Margaret." Uncle Will stopped and sighed. "My mother was from Boston and she'd never met anybody like Dad, at least that's what she told me. They were married, and I was born soon after. For years, Dad couldn't seem to hold down a steady job, so they decided to move back here to work things out. My mother wasn't used to the country, but she grew to love it. Dad, on the other hand, seemed to hold a grudge against anybody who wanted to work the land. He didn't get along with Grandpa. The rest of us were caught in the middle. We stayed here for a few years, helping out on the ranch, but Dad and Grandpa fought all the time, although maybe it wasn't what you'd call fighting. It was more like stony silence. I learned to work in silence, and got to enjoy it. If there was silence, I could pretend nothing was wrong." Uncle Will paused. I stared at him. I'd never heard him say this much at one time.

"One day Dad couldn't take it anymore. He told Mom he was leaving to find a way to support us elsewhere. He left us with my grandparents, even though Mom begged him not to go or to wait until we could all leave together. He refused. And was gone, just like that." There was a hard note in Uncle Will's voice that I'd never heard.

"We waited for years, only hearing from Dad on occasion, until the day he showed up. I was twelve. By this time I had been working with Grandpa every day, and he was showing me how to run the ranch. I loved the work and hated every memory I had of city life— living in tiny apartments in dirty neighborhoods and attending loud, rowdy schools. Dad knew I'd changed the moment he saw me, and he hated it. He forced me to do what a twelve-year-old should never have to do. He made me choose." Uncle Will raised his hat with his right hand, wiping his forehead with his upper arm.

After resettling his hat, he stared off so long I thought he was done. Then he said, "Dad took me out for a ride in his new car. 'Look, Will,' he said, 'out there as far as you can see is pastureland. There's no future here, only grass and heartache. I've lived here longer than you and I've seen how this place destroys people. Away from here is a different world—industry, life, adventure! We can live far away from this dead place!'

"He had a way of speaking that drew people in, but I fought

against his words. I couldn't believe that this place was as terrible as he said. He seemed to realize I didn't agree. 'Will, you're my son. You should be with your father,' he said. 'What about Mom?' I asked. 'Of course she'll come too.' 'I want to talk to Mom,' I said.

"We both talked to Mom. She wanted to know if he had a home for us. Dad was evasive, then admitted he didn't. 'You left when we didn't want you to,' she said, 'and now you come back without a place for us to go?' Mom had grown to love the ranch and she wanted Dad and Grandpa to be reconciled. Dad got angry. He turned to me and I could feel the power of his charm. 'Will,' he said, 'would you rather go with me and have great adventures or stay here and follow this old man's rules?' 'I want to be with Mom,' I said. I was loyal to her because she had never deserted me, and had stayed with me in North Dakota, a place far from where she grew up, waiting for Dad.

"He was disgusted. 'What'll it be, Will?' he asked. 'I like it here,' was all I could get out. He left that day and never came back. My mother was never the same, though at times she seemed happier than she'd been before. She taught me so much. You may have seen her name in some of the books I have. They were hers."

I saw in my mind the neat cursive name—*Margaret Smith*—written in the flyleaf of some of his books.

Uncle Will sighed. "Grandpa taught me everything he knew about ranching and about life. I've always been grateful to him for that."

We sat in silence. I wanted to reach out and touch his arm. *He understands! He lost a father too!* Uncle Will's young horse shifted under him until at last he clucked to the horse and we moved on down into the ravine.

Chapter
8

I felt even more isolated from my classmates during my junior year of high school. Most of them treated me like a social misfit. They were willing to accept an outsider, but my continued reserve alienated them. Now they seemed to enjoy teasing and mocking me. I didn't mind because I was usually amused by their attempts to offend me. However, sometimes the raillery would get to me, and I was relieved to hear the ringing of the last bell of the day. On days like that, all I wanted to do was spend time in the silence of the barn with the horses, absorbing their animal strength and patience.

One day at school was worse than most. I'd endured an icy coldness all day and wanted to get out of there. I saw Aunt Bea's pickup in the yard when I returned to the ranch, even though she was supposed to be at work. She and Uncle Will were in the pasture behind the barn examining a horse that was lying on its side on the ground. I dropped my books inside the door and ran to see what was up. It was Belle on the ground, and she was moaning with each breath.

"What's wrong?" I asked.

Aunt Bea sighed and ran her hands through her hair. "I'm afraid she's broken a leg."

"You can fix it."

"No, dear. It's too bad and she's too old."

Uncle Will squatted and stroked Belle's neck. "Hey, hey, old girl," he said, "we'll take care of you."

I knelt by her head and stroked her face, remembering she was the first horse I had seen when I arrived. She lifted her head and tried to get up.

"Easy, Belle," I said, pressing down on her neck. "Lie still." She rolled her eyes and laid her head back down with a groan.

"Isn't there anything we can do?" I said. My tongue felt heavy forming the words.

"We have to put her to sleep," Aunt Bea said, and put her hand on my shoulder. I shrugged it off, and said, "That's not fair!"

"Life's not always fair, honey," she said.

I snorted and turned back to Belle. Uncle Will was stroking her neck and shoulder and murmuring to her. His hat was off, sitting upside down on the ground next to him. He looked vulnerable, somehow, without his hat. The wind stirred his hair, except for the smooth band where his hat had rested.

Aunt Bea was standing by us with a huge syringe. I felt a grip to my throat difficult to swallow past. Uncle Will looked up at her and nodded. Belle didn't flinch as the needle slipped into her vein, but I couldn't watch as Aunt Bea injected the lethal dose. The indefinable glow of life faded from Belle's eyes, until they were blank and glassy. She wasn't breathing.

Uncle Will ran his hand through her thick red mane one last time. "Well, Belle," he said, "You were always a sweet girl. And we had some adventures, didn't we?" He stood and rested his hand on my head. "She had a good life."

I straightened her forelock with my trembling hands and stood, shaking like I had during the darkness of that storm. Belle looked like an empty skin stuffed with sawdust.

I turned and ran through the pasture. I heard Aunt Bea call after me. I kept running until I collapsed under a bare tree at the base of a hill. I couldn't catch my breath, and it wasn't from running. There was a choking feeling in my throat and my eyes burned. My chest felt ready to burst. I lay on my stomach, beat the ground with my fists, and gained control of my breathing. The dry grass sighed and hissed around me as the wind swished through it.

I rolled over and focused on the grass and the sky above. Fall had arrived and I hadn't realized it. I could feel the evening chill descending on me, yet I still felt the warmth of the long, hazy afternoon in the ground where I lay. I could smell the straw-like smell of sun-cured grass, and the drying leaves of the tree above rattled together in the fading evening breeze. I closed my eyes. An autumn laziness was dragging me down into the darkness. I breathed deep. My heartbeat slowed.

I opened my eyes and saw it was almost dark. Oliver was lying in the brown grass beside me. When he saw me look at him, he whined and pawed at my leg.

"Come on, Ollie, let's go back."

He barked and leaped ahead, turning to see if I was following. It was dark by the time I reached the house. I went in the front door and heard Aunt Bea pacing in the kitchen, talking to Uncle Will.

"I'm telling you, Will, I'm worried. It's dark and she was upset."

"She can take care of herself."

Uncle Will sounded tired, as if this conversation had been going on for a while.

"I know, but she was really upset. She was so interested in being a vet. Now this."

"Now she knows the stakes," he said, and I realized that it had been hard for him to lose Belle, too, as he had. I went in to the kitchen, and Aunt Bea cried out and hugged me. Uncle Will walked over, laid his hand on my shoulder, and looked down at me with a sad, tired smile. He walked past and went to their bedroom.

"Aunt Bea, I've made up my mind. I want to be a veterinarian," I said, and walked away, hearing her startled "Oh!" behind me.

Two days later, on a Sunday, I went to church with Uncle Will and Aunt Bea as usual, and stared at the back of the pew in front of us, clenching my teeth together during the songs until there was silence in my head. I hated going to church. The music was bad enough, but I was also aggravated by people who tried talking to me. *Why do they want to know about my life anyway? Can't they leave me alone?*

I was in a bad mood every Sunday until I could concentrate and wipe everything out and hear only echoing silence. Uncle Will and Aunt Bea never talked to me about it, but I sensed they knew my feelings. I went to church because I knew it was important to them, even though they didn't make any attempt to coerce me into going. So I kept going, and I hated it.

But this Sunday was worse than most. Not only was I still upset about Belle, but this was a Sunday when the church choir sang, in addition to the usual hymns. I concentrated so hard on blocking out the music that I had a headache when we left the church building.

I said I was going to my room when we got back to the house.

"Are you all right?" Aunt Bea asked.

"Yes. I have a headache and I'm tired, that's all. And I'm not hungry."

"Okay, honey, you should probably rest then."

Uncle Will looked at me, his clear eyes darkening. He said nothing, turning away to hang up his hat as I went upstairs.

I didn't sleep. I lay on my bed and looked out the window, my pulse beating in my head. The light blurred and seemed to flicker, and I blinked several times, but it wasn't my eyes. A sudden early-autumn whirl of snow had descended on the landscape. I sat up, thinking it was rare that the weather suited a person's mood.

I had to go outside to watch the snow.

"Gabe, where are you going?" Aunt Bea asked.

"I think some fresh air will help my headache."

Uncle Will held a book, his head bent down, but looking up at me from under his eyebrows.

"Well," Aunt Bea said, "don't go too far."

"I won't."

The power of the wind driving the snow exhilarated me. I stood in the yard, watching the ground gradually grow submerged in soft flakes. Every now and then the wind would let up for a moment, and the diagonal drive of the flakes would lift into swirls that were driven into the ground when the wind returned.

I walked toward the tree rows, relishing the sting of snow on my face. In the shelter of the trees, the snow fell in such straight lines it settled on my hair like goose down. The tops of the trees swayed and groaned as the wind passed through them. I stood in the quiet below, watching the trees' animation in the wind and snow.

I knew how unpredictable winter was here. The cold could be subzero or it might snow and rain the same day. The ferocity of the wind could sometimes surprise me—I had thought I knew about wind, living in Chicago, which was, after all, "The Windy City." But the wind on the plains had nothing much to stop it or break its flow. So it gathered speed, blasting around or through anything that got in the way. Some days it felt like the wind had gone through me until there was nothing left inside except cold. I felt I was bit by bit being turned into a statue of ice.

I had come to love the ferocity of the storms. There was a kind of unexplainable peace in the middle of the howling cold and lashing snow. My spirit always seemed to rise to meet the onslaught of the weather. This feeling returned now as I saw the early snow devouring the brown ground, as if greedy for grass and dirt. The snow was freezing onto the trees, burdening them with white tentacles of frost. I laughed. I felt full of the savagery I could see all around. I knew the sun would win the battle tomorrow, that the snow would fall in sodden heaps from the drooping branches of the trees, but now, in the middle of the swirl of white, I was alone, watching the icy blue light slide into dark blue, the trees luminescent in their white coats, the wind singing its hoarse victory song. *Oblivion. Oblivion.* It was the song I wanted to hear.

Chapter
9

$\mathcal{I}$ focused more on my science classes at school and started looking at colleges that offered pre-vet degrees. Aunt Bea and Uncle Will had never saved to send a child to college—and I didn't expect it from them—so I looked for ways to save money. One college particularly interested me since it was in-state. That would lower the cost, and it offered good scholarships.

I started studying for the SAT and ACT tests and kept my grades high. So at high school I was now a brain, as well as antisocial. It bothered the other students that I didn't engage in their pastimes of cruising around, going to parties, hanging out, or shopping.

I entered my senior year self-labeled as an outcast, and that enabled me to focus more energy on my studies. I looked at some other school-related activities at the recommendation of one of my teachers, who said colleges look at that as well as transcripts. Uncle Will had gotten me involved in 4-H horse shows, and now I joined the track team. All the physical work I'd done with Uncle Will had strengthened me and given me endurance.

My coach tried me out on various events and found that I was able to run distances at a good pace. I alienated most of my track teammates because I was never late to practices or meets, and never complained about the rigorous conditioning. The difference between me and my teammates was simple—I hated wasting time on frivolity. And when I was running, I could press past pain and fatigue. I could tap into strength deep in me, a primitive force I didn't want to see or name.

I was eighteen when I graduated from high school, would turn nineteen soon, and had been living with my aunt and uncle for a little over three years. The graduation ceremony was long and tedious. I would have been happy getting my diploma in the mail.

As I was on my way out to meet Uncle Will and Aunt Bea after the ceremony, Kim, one of my classmates, approached me. She had been the friendliest when I first started school.

"Uh, Gabrielle," she said.

"Yes?" I said.

"I was wondering," she said. "Well, you see, I'm having a grad party tonight and I think everyone's coming and I wanted to invite you because it's going to be lots of fun."

"Yeah, maybe I could come. Where is it?"

"Oh, it's gonna be so *cool!* The party is at my parents' place, at eight, down by the river. Please come!"

"I think I can, for a while. Should I bring anything?"

"Oh! Awesome! Just bring a sweatshirt or something warm. Oh, and maybe bug spray."

"Okay, sounds good." I didn't know why I had agreed to go, but I was too far in to back out now, so I got directions from Kim. After filling me in, she smiled, then ran off to join her friends.

Uncle Will and Aunt Bea were waiting for me outside the school building. Aunt Bea smothered me in a hug, and I could see she'd been crying.

"Oh, Gabe, we are so proud of you!" she cried. She released me and smoothed my hair.

Uncle Will hugged me also. "You've done real well, Gabrielle," he said, and smiled down at me, his shining blue eyes full of pride.

I pulled up to Kim's party just as the long twilight of spring was beginning. Most of the senior class and a lot of juniors were there. They had a bonfire going and were roasting hot dogs and marshmallows. Most of them were drinking beer. I wished I hadn't come, but I got out of my car and walked toward the fire. Kim saw me and ran over. I could hear her giggling before she got close.

"I'm so glad you came, Gabrielle!" she said, giggling again. "I think I'm a little tipsy!"

I stuck my hands in my jeans' pockets.

"Come on!" Kim pulled me over to the bonfire and made me sit beside her on a log rolled close. Some of the kids were loud, unsteady, and glassy-eyed. Duncan was there, but seemed his usual laconic self.

"Hey, kid," Duncan said, "are you happy to be gradumacated?"

"Yes."

"Yep, me too. I'm done with school. I want to run the ranch. I have ideas, but I'll have to duke it out with my dad. Should be fun, huh?" He grinned down at me. I smiled back, and thought, *He's more grown up than any of our classmates.*

"You're going off to college somewhere, aren'tcha?"

"Yes," I said.

"Well, good for you!" Duncan ran his arm around my shoulders. "You'll go far! Don't forget where you came from, though."

Chicago? I thought, but his kindness and sincerity affected me more than I cared to show. "Thanks, Duncan. Make sure you get your dad to listen to your ideas."

"Hey, Duncan!" someone yelled from the other side of the fire. "Is she your girlfriend? I thought you had better taste!"

"Piss off, ya pig-headed son of a sheep-farmer!" Duncan yelled back. "People are dumb," he said to me and went in the direction of the insulter. I watched him go, wondering if I'd see him again.

Derek, a popular track-team star, called to me across the fire. "Hey, Gabrielle, how does it feel to be the biggest brain in school?" His buddies laughed, so he continued. "I mean, I was just gonna tell

you to stay standing up front during graduation, because you got all
the awards anyhoo!"

Kim nudged me. "He's been drinking, ignore him." She giggled
again. "He's just jealous," she said in a loud voice, to make sure Derek
heard. "He doesn't know how anyone can be that smart because *he*
isn't, that's for sure!"

Derek frowned and sat down and his buddies howled with
laughter.

I turned over a marshmallow Kim had given me to roast, wondering if my face was hot from the fire or Derek's teasing. Duncan
called to Kim from the edge of the firelight, and she went to talk to
him. I felt a chill settle over my shoulders, even though the fire out-
lined all of my exposed skin with warmth.

I stayed until it was pitch-black, so no one would notice me leaving. The girls around me were huddled close, whispering, and I figured they were talking about me. I left the uneven ring of light cast
by the fire and stumbled through the dark, grass twisting around
my ankles as I headed in the direction of my car. I heard footsteps
behind me, and turned. I expected Duncan, but it was Derek.

"Hey, Gabrielle, sorry about teasing you. It's cool to be smart."

"Sure, okay."

He stared at me a minute and shifted his weight.

"Are you leaving already?" he asked.

"Yes."

"Hey, um, why don't you stay? We could talk, or something."

"About what?"

"Uh, I dunno. Just talk, I guess."

"I don't exactly feel welcome here," I said.

"Whose fault is that, da ya think?"

"Excuse me? I'm leaving."

"Wait." Derek put his hand on my arm. "I'm sorry again. I

shouldn'ta said that. I guess I've had a little too much to drink." He laughed, embarrassed.

"Well," I said, "that's a real recommendation for staying and talking to you."

His hand slipped from my arm. "You know what's funny?" he said. "I've liked you since the day you got here. I admired your courage and your talent." He paused, and I noticed him shaking his head in the darkness. "You would be beautiful if you weren't such a bitch."

I watched him walk away until he faded in the dark. He was steady on his feet. *How can my ears be ringing when his voice was quiet?*

I got into my car and sat for a while.

Bitch? Am I that awful? You have to get drunk to say that to me, Derek?

I slammed my hand down on the steering wheel.

What right does he have to judge me? He has no clue!

I drove around on the back roads until my thoughts were under control.

When I pulled into the driveway I saw that Uncle Will and Aunt Bea had left a light on for me. I went in the back door to the kitchen to get a drink of water. Uncle Will was still up, reading *The Brothers Karamazov* at the kitchen table. He looked up and smiled.

"So, you're back," he said, and turned aside to his book.

I poured myself some water and sat down at the table.

How did he know I needed silence?

I watched his eyes move over the pages as he read, his hand smoothing his mustache from time to time. I went over to him and bent down and kissed his cheek. He looked at me, startled, then smiled and squeezed my hand pressed on the edge of the table.

"Goodnight, Gabrielle."

"Goodnight, Uncle Will."

I walked out of the kitchen and turned at the doorway to see he had returned to his book. He was smiling.

Chapter
10

$\mathcal{I}$ had been accepted to my school of choice, Jamestown College, in the mid-eastern part of the state, but was waiting to see if I would get a scholarship or two. I had high scores on the ACT and SAT and had sent off essays for scholarships, so all I could do was wait.

I received a packet, after several weeks, informing me that I had received the second highest scholarship, which would cover two-thirds of the cost of school. Aunt Bea was more excited than I was. I was relieved—it was that much less I would have to pay.

That summer I got a day job at the local grocery store to earn spending money for college. This helped me buy clothes and other supplies I would need. In the evenings I worked with Uncle Will, helping him make hay and riding young, not fully trained horses, which he referred to as "green."

August came, and my birthday drew near. The sunrise on the seventeenth sent out hard, pink streaks into a light-blue sky. It was clear and cloudless, and I knew it was going to be hot. I dressed and went down to the kitchen.

"Happy birthday, Gabrielle!" Aunt Bea said, giving me a hug and a kiss on the cheek.

"Happy birthday!" Uncle Will said, and smiled at me.

"Thanks." I smiled back at them both. I found it hard to believe that I was nineteen and starting college in two weeks.

"I made your favorite blueberry pancakes, and Will fried up

some bacon and eggs," Aunt Bea said, and then pushed me over to the table. "Now you just sit and eat and I'll serve you."

When I was done, Aunt Bea cleared my plate and laid a large present on the table in front of me.

"Open it," she said.

Inside was an afghan, knitted in red with white and green accents, in a pattern similar to paintings of Norwegian rosemaling Aunt Bea had shown me once.

"It's beautiful! Did you make it?" I ran my hands over it, feeling the texture created by the twisted patterns of yarn.

She nodded. "I thought it would be something homey you could take to college with you."

"It's great!" I said.

"I'm glad you like it." She began picking up the wrapping paper. I put the afghan on the couch in the living room, then came back into the kitchen.

"I was thinking that I would go for a ride this morning," I told them, "before it gets too hot."

"Good idea," Uncle Will said. "You do that. I'll take care of the chores."

I put on my boots and went out to the barn. Some of the horses were at the back of the barn drinking water. I caught one of them, a six-year-old buckskin gelding named Eagle. He had a white blaze that passed over his left eye, and that eye was blue. The eye appeared watchful, predatory almost, so Uncle Will let me name him Eagle. The name was ironic because he was a sweet and gentle horse, and became one of my favorites for ranch work.

I led Eagle into a stall beside the tack room and started brushing him. He sighed with contentment and cocked a hind leg, resting his weight on three. I brushed his dark-gold coat, and his black mane and tail. I put my face against his neck and inhaled. I would miss that smell when I was at school—the smell of hair swept by wind and grass—a sweet, dusty, lemony, and salty smell. Uncle Will was opening and closing stalls and leading horses around. He came over just as I finished tacking up Eagle.

"Before you go, I want to show you something."

"All right." I finished buckling the bridle and followed him to a stall.

Uncle Will stopped in front of it and turned to me. "Inside the stall is your birthday present from me," he said. As I looked in, he added, "She's five months old."

She was a bay filly—each hair a shining, golden red—with solid black legs and a narrow, crooked white blaze ending just above her black-rimmed nostrils. She looked back at me, her eyes calm and warm, her small, black-tipped ears turning in her fuzzy mane. She was beautiful. I couldn't believe that Uncle Will said she was mine.

"I got her from a horse trainer I know," he said. "Her registered name is Leo's Bar Anita, but they called her Anita. She's got some great cow-horse bloodlines."

I could feel him looking at me, but I was speechless. I stretched my hand over the side of the stall and the filly sniffed it, then lipped it with her soft, fuzzy mouth.

Uncle Will is giving her to me!

An ache started in my chest and my throat tightened. This was the best gift I had ever received since my parents' death. I felt a prickling sensation at the back of my eyes. A stab of white-hot pain shot through me and made me gasp.

No! I gripped the side of the stall. *I won't break down, I won't lose control!*

I could feel myself flush, and before I knew it I was staring at Uncle Will. "This is a bribe to try to keep me here," I said. "It won't work. I'm leaving, and you can take her back. I don't want her!"

I saw the look of shock and pain in Uncle Will's eyes, but I ran to Eagle and led him out of the barn. It took a moment for me to climb on. Eagle was moving in a circle, picking his hooves up in a mincing dance and snorting—he'd sensed my blind fury. Once I was in the saddle, we galloped away.

I don't know how long it was before Eagle's rhythmic strides and the wind stinging my face brought me to my senses, but at last I realized how fast we were going. I stopped Eagle and slid off, clinging to his mane, shaking. He turned his head to me, black-rimmed nostrils stretched so wide with his breathing I could see the pink membranes in his nose. Eagle nudged me with his nose, his blue eye wide.

"I'm sorry," I said, and smoothed his mane until my shaking stopped and his breathing slowed. I mounted again and we went on at a walk. It was midmorning before I turned around and went back, so it was noon before I topped a hill and saw the ranch yard below, shimmering mirage-like in the heat waves rising from the ground. The grass underfoot smelled like cured hay, the dusty smell of autumn come too soon.

I stopped Eagle and stared at the barn. I nudged him and we went down the hill. The tick of Eagle's hooves on the gravel drive in the still, oppressive heat sounded ominous. I dismounted and led him into the same stall I used earlier.

I took my time unsaddling him and brushing him down. His coat was crusted with dried sweat, so I led him to a spigot on the other side of the barn, and hosed him down until he gleamed, his coat slick with water. I put him back in the stall and gave him some oats. I paused at the barn door and stared at the house, no longer able to avoid the inevitable.

What am I going to say?

I sighed and walked toward the house, staring at the ground and noticing details in it for the first time.

PAST DARKNESS

We ate lunch in a silence as ominous as the oppressive heat out-side. Even Aunt Bea said nothing. I looked up at Uncle Will and saw him staring at his plate and eating in a mechanical manner. I knew I needed to apologize, but I couldn't form the words. What I said was worse than Derek's slap at me.

I went to the barn to let Eagle out as soon as lunch was over. I avoided looking in any of the other stalls as I led him out of the barn. I turned him back out in the pasture and watched as he dropped down and rolled in the grass, grunting with pleasure as he rubbed his back on the ground, his hooves and legs thrashing the air.

"Sure, ruin the nice grooming job I did." My words sounded dead in the hot air.

Eagle got up and trotted out to join a group of horses in the distance.

"Gabrielle!" Aunt Bea was calling from inside the barn. I went back inside. "Oh, there you are. I have to go out on a call for some-one I know. Want to come?"

"Yes."

"Well then, let's go."

We climbed into her vet pickup that she had pulled up, run-ning, in front of the barn, and drove about ten miles on gravel roads, before pulling into a farmyard. A man came from the house to meet us, followed by a young girl who was obviously upset.

"So, Sasha," Aunt Bea said, "I hear your pony is hurt."

Sasha nodded and bit her lip, close to tears.

"Well, I'm sure we can fix Licorice in no time!" Aunt Bea lifted her heavy medical bag from the pickup with the ease of practice. We followed Sasha and her father to a pen where a fat brown-black pony stood. He had a deep cut on his chest that was dripping blood.

"Oofda," Aunt Bea said. "Gabe, will you hold his head for me?"

76

I held the pony's halter with one hand and rubbed his forehead with the other while Aunt Bea examined the wound.

"Terry, do you know how this happened?" Aunt Bea asked.

"Well, I just got a new horse and I figure she probably kicked him."

"Yes, that seems right. I'll give him a shot of local anesthesia and stitch him up. It isn't too deep into the muscle tissue and should heal fine."

"That's great," Terry said. "Isn't it, Sasha?"

Sasha nodded, her brown eyes wide and solemn. She buried her face in Terry's side as Aunt Bea pulled out a needle and syringe.

Aunt Bea injected anesthesia into the area around the wound, and we waited until it was numb. She applied an antiseptic and stitched the muscle and then the skin together. She applied antiseptic and fly spray to the area around the wound.

"Terry, you should keep him by himself for a while," Aunt Bea said, "so the wound can heal. But make sure he moves around. If he develops a fever or in any way acts strange, call me. Otherwise, that should do it!"

"Thank you so much," Terry said. "How much do I owe you?"

"Oh, nothing," Aunt Bea said. "This is just a favor for a friend. I wanted to help Licorice. Do you think he looks better now, honey?"

"Oh, yes," Sasha said. "Thank you!" She rubbed Licorice's nose.

We left after a little small talk. I was sure Uncle Will told Aunt Bea about my outburst, and I was waiting in dread for her to bring it up.

"Do you know much about your grandparents, my parents?" Aunt Bea asked.

I was surprised. "No," I said.

"My father was strong, solid, and proud—so proud he wouldn't admit it was a bad idea to farm in western North Dakota, instead of raising stock maybe more suited to the landscape. He and Mom got married later in life, so they were older than most of my friends' parents."

I figured this had something to do with how I should have responded to Uncle Will. But I was glad to let her keep talking as long as her talk didn't veer toward me. "What was your mom like?" I asked.

"She was sensible and funny. She taught me how to make lefse and rosettes. She also had that gift with animals, though not as much as her mother. Grandma's the one who talked to them in Norwegian."

"Cool," I said, and hoped she would keep going.

"My parents were *very* Norwegian—my maiden name is Iverson, for goodness' sake—even though they were also, oh, such Americans. They loved the old traditions, but they also knew when to let them go and focus on America. Sometimes I wonder if young people realize how much they could learn from generations who lived so differently."

Here it comes, I thought.

"People understood hard work and perseverance, those necessities," Aunt Bea said, in a dark tone. She turned in the driveway to the ranch, and I was relieved that she hadn't brought up the incident yet. At least now she would not be able to keep me captive for long if she started to berate me. She pulled up to the house and stopped the pickup and turned to me with a smile, as if our entire conversation had been commonplace. I smiled back and stepped out of the pickup, even though I was curious now about my grandparents and wanted to ask her more.

I received a birthday card from my Chicago friend Carmen that afternoon, and it filled me with guilt. I hadn't responded to her long letters, and she had stopped writing. Now I only heard from her at Christmas and on my birthday. I would respond to her cards, but it was a polite response. Not what Carmen wanted, I knew.

I spent the rest of the day in my room. My excuse was that I was organizing for college. In reality, I wanted to avoid Uncle Will and any conversation that Aunt Bea might start about this morning. Carmen's card was also weighing on my mind, so any excuse to be alone seemed valid.

Aunt Bea presented me with a chocolate cake at dinner. Once again, we were all quiet, and, after helping clean up, I went to my room, saying I was tired and wanted to get to bed early. But I lay awake, listening to the moaning of the wind through the trees, the first breeze of the day, and the far-off grumble of thunder.

I woke up several hours later, knowing something was wrong. It took me a minute to realize what it was—perfect, ear-aching silence. Suddenly I could see myself from above, and I was tiny and alone in a huge emptiness. I closed my eyes, but it seemed I was forever falling into endless dark. I tried to move or make a sound, but I was paralyzed by fear. I had never felt so alone.

When I heard the faint moaning of the wind again, I was able to move and look out the window. My room was the sticky black of tar pitch. I could see the outline of the window. The sky outside was deep blue, showing the sparkle of stars. I stared out the window at those stars until my eyes ached. The terror subsided, and I fell into an exhausted sleep.

I spent the time before college staying out of Uncle Will's way when I could. There seemed an unspoken agreement between us to avoid each other. Uncle Will never asked me to help with anything. If I was in the barn or with one of the horses, he would leave and not return until I left. I was relieved—at least I didn't have to pretend nothing had happened. I knew Uncle Will was too honest for that anyway.

I gathered and organized the last of the necessities I would need for school. The day arrived when I had to leave to make it to campus in time for freshman orientation, so we loaded up the cars. The original plan was that we would all go in two cars, but at the last minute, Uncle Will said he had to finish haying and couldn't go. This seemed a rather transparent excuse to me, yet I was ashamed at my relief.

As Aunt Bea was inside getting her purse, Uncle Will came over to me. I stood next to my car, ignoring his approach, hoping he would walk by without speaking to me. This time I was wrong. He stopped in front of me and stood a moment, hesitating.

He reached out, took my left hand, and put a book into it. "Something for you to read," he said, "in any free moments, if you have any."

I stared at the book, Homer's *The Odyssey*. He put his hands on my shoulders and I looked up. His eyes were level and kind.

"I love you, Gabrielle," he said, and I could feel my face flushing red. "You're on your own odyssey now."

I stared at him in silence. I realized he had been avoiding me because he was aware that's what I wanted. Still, I said nothing. He shook me once, let his hands go, and walked over to say goodbye to Aunt Bea. I got in my car, closed the door, and sat still as a statue. I felt numbing prickles in my hands and feet.

Aunt Bea followed me during the five-hour trip east. Once we arrived at the college, it was easy for me to find my dorm since I remembered the campus from a tour I'd taken earlier. We carried my belongings to my room and saw that my roommate's were already there.

She came in a few minutes later and introduced herself. "Hi! You must be Gabrielle. I'm Alicia Porter, your new roommate!" She was short and petite with long, red-gold hair. She had a firm grip and sparkling green eyes.

"I'm so glad to finally meet you, and I'm so excited to be here. You'll have to forgive me if I talk too much!" She spoke without pausing for breath, leaning forward in enthusiasm.

I introduced Aunt Bea, and they began chatting as I brought in the last few articles from my car.

Aunt Bea had to get back to home, back to work. She held me tight for a long minute.

"I'm going to miss you *so much*, Gabrielle! You'll have to write and call, and I promise to do the same."

"I will."

She wiped her eyes. "Well, I'd better go before I really start crying." She laughed and gave me another squeeze before climbing in her car.

"Keep in touch!" she said, leaning out the window, and then she drove away. I stood on the sidewalk, watching her go, and felt nothing.

Chapter
11

$\mathcal{J}$amestown College was similar to high school. Alicia attempted to befriend me, but gave up after a while, and we went our separate ways. What she and the rest of my classmates didn't understand was that I didn't like people to befriend me.

I didn't want them analyzing my face and emotions. I even hated looking in mirrors—I saw too much of my parents in my reflection. I had my mother's unruly hair and my father's hazel eyes. Recognizing their features terrified me, so I avoided mirrors as much as possible. I didn't want friends either, because I heard myself talking to others in the voices of my parents and couldn't stand that. I needed my own voice, which I found easiest in silence. So my life included my studies and my conscious avoidance of people.

But there was a sense of community at Jamestown College that I felt both isolated from and drawn to. That the college was small didn't mean the classes were easy. The teachers took time to get to know each student and in return expected respect and effort from them in their classes. I did as well in academics as I had in high school.

I almost never returned to the ranch, even though it was only about five hours away. I rarely wrote or called, and only went back for a few major holidays. My sophomore year I became a resident assistant so I could have my own room and also an excuse to stay on campus nearly full time. I was an RA for a dorm that housed most of the international students, which worked well for me because they couldn't talk to me too much.

I had been bothered before, and was again, by the study habits of fellow students. Many of them listened to music while studying, and it blared through the halls and stairwells. I couldn't stand this, so I studied in the library as much as I could. When I couldn't do that, I sat in my room wearing earplugs, so I could study in silence.

I found jobs in Jamestown over the summers, also, and only went back to the ranch for vacations. So I graduated with honors, went to vet school in Iowa, and returned to the ranch even less. More years passed and I graduated again, and found a job in Jamestown. I had grown familiar with Jamestown and liked it there. I no longer enjoyed the constant rush of big-city life, and Jamestown combined city and small-town feeling into one. I appreciated the setting and was glad I had the opportunity to work there, for now at least.

The clinic where I got a job was run by a pair of women veterinarians—Dr. Lintock, who was near retirement, and Dr. Swimmley. They hoped I would gain experience before Dr. Lintock retired. They had a vet tech, Tracy, who reminded me of my former roommate, Alicia. Tracy was short and petite, too, but she had shorn black hair and fawn-like amber eyes. She was friendly, and we worked well together. Half of my first year working as a vet was over when I realized I hadn't been to the ranch once.

Chapter
12

*T*racy burst into the clinic one day, half an hour late, face glowing.

"You're late," Dr. Lintock said.

"I know, I'm so sorry," Tracy said, "but I've got some great news!" She was flushed and smiling. "You all know my boyfriend, Jason, right? Well, he just proposed!"

"Well! Congratulations!" Dr. Swimmley said. "No wonder you're late!"

"The ring?" Dr. Lintock said.

Tracy held out her hand, bearing a new ring for our admiration.

When Tracy and I were working in the back later, she said, "Jason's parents are throwing an engagement party soon, and I would really like you to come."

"I don't know, Tracy," I said. I hated such events. People always asked me if I had a boyfriend and sighed in sympathy when I said no. They never bothered to ask if I *wanted* a boyfriend. Guess what? I didn't.

"*Please*, Gabrielle." Tracy's fawn-like eyes were difficult to resist. "Jason has a lot of friends and they'll all be there. I don't have many friends around here and it would be so nice if you would come, even if only for a little while."

I knew she would keep after me until the party, so I gave in. "Okay, when will it be?" I asked.

"Oh, *thank you!*" Tracy said, and hugged me. "It will probably be on a Friday, at the local community center, I guess. Jason's mom is so excited, *she* wants to do all the arrangement herself." She sighed and rolled her eyes. "Oh well, less for me to do, right? Anyway, it will be after work. I'll let you know the exact day and time when everything is finalized. I'm so glad you're going to come!" She moved away with such an airy walk I almost checked to see if her feet were touching the ground. I shook my head.

I admitted my loneliness for the first time in a long time as I sat alone in my apartment that night. I stared at the phone, debating whether I should call Uncle Will and Aunt Bea. Emptiness spread through me like an invading thief. I saw a notebook on the table and pulled it to me. I closed my eyes and smelled the herbal smell of warm grass and sage, the exotic orange scent of Russian-olive trees, the salty-sweet odor of horses, and the pithy smell of dirt torn up by hooves. And I could hear the watery whispering hiss of the wind over the grassy plain, the cries of coyotes, the liquid warble of a meadowlark, the keening cry of a hawk, and the tattling sound of cottonwood leaves rattling against others in a summer breeze.

I saw gray-white clouds pile their rainy masses on the horizon, the swaying purple dance of summer lilacs in a high wind, the way a mare and colt could run in perfect step, the shine of light off Aunt Bea's needles, and Uncle Will's silhouette as he sat horseback against a sunset streaking the west with purple, orange, and pink.

I felt the barbed heads of crested wheatgrass catch my jeans, the rounded pain of gravel under my bare feet, the silky prickle of a horse's nose-skin studded with whiskers, the satin swipe of Ollie's tongue, the feel of wind tugging my hair, and the hide-bound, rippled-muscle feel of riding a horse bareback.

I flipped open the notebook and began writing:

In the falling rain I heard you calling me,
In the driving snow I heard you calling me.

But where are you now?
In the seething fire I heard you calling me,
In the rushing wind I heard you calling me.
But where are you now?
In the mourning dove's cry I heard you calling me,
In the thunder I heard you call.
But where are you now?
Why did you leave me alone?
The falling rain's my unshed tears,
The driving snow is like my thoughts.
Where are you?
The seething fire becomes my heart,
The rushing wind becomes my soul.
Where are you?
The mourning dove's cry is my own cry,
The thunder unleashes the riot of my fear.
Where are you?
Why did you leave me alone?
Nature is the echo of my emptiness.
I am alone.

I stared at what I wrote and shivered. I slammed my notebook shut and stuffed it under some medical textbooks and went to bed.

I was standing outside a community center two weeks later, wishing I were anywhere else but here. I could hear people talking and laughing inside, and I sighed. This was going to be miserable. I drew my shoulders back, clenched my jaw, and entered. The place was decorated with balloons and banners and packed with milling, talking people. I saw Tracy and Jason surrounded by a crowd and didn't want to push through them all to talk to Tracy, so I headed for the far side of the room—a dim area I saw near the right corner of a stage. I sat down at a table there just as the lights went out. A spotlight came on at the other side of the stage. A man stood in the light with a microphone.

"Hello," he said. "You don't all know me, but I'm Jason's father, and I'm here to say congratulations to the happy couple!" The room exploded with clapping, stomping, and ear-splitting whistles. "Yes, I know," he said, "we are all happy for them. But instead of boring you with stories and talk, I am going to introduce another fine young man. His name is Ian Mackenzie, a friend of both Tracy's and Jason's from way back, and he's going to play the violin for us tonight."

There was another burst of applause as the spotlight shifted to center stage. A man was standing there, chestnut-red hair falling across his forehead, a violin in his left hand, bow in his right, and a microphone in front of him.

I stood up, thinking, *Idiot! Of course they'd have entertainment! Why did I come? I have to get out of here!*

Something about the way the musician inclined his head to the applause and stepped up to the microphone stopped me. I stood undecided.

I can always leave.

"I will be playing a few of my own compositions for you tonight," the musician said. He had an arresting voice, quiet yet assured, and I sat down.

"The first song I will play was inspired by my life experiences, and I call it 'Music to My Eyes.'"

He took a step back from the microphone and lifted the violin to his shoulder, holding the bow poised above the strings for a moment, and then leaned forward and began playing. The first notes vibrated in my chest, mesmerizing me. His playing was slow, but picked up speed—my eyes were drawn to the dance of his fingers over the strings. His hair fell across his forehead, glowing scarlet against his spotlight-paled skin. The melody was light and fast, rollicking, and so full of joy I started choking.

I noticed a difference after a while—the song wasn't happy any longer; it was frenzied. It was building to a catastrophe, faster and faster until with a horrible screech, silence. I could feel the tension in the room, a pause of awed anticipation. My nerves felt laid bare and raw. Then from the violin came a low mournful moaning. It was the sound of hopeless despair, and I couldn't bear it. I tried to stand but the strength left my legs, and I fell back in the chair, my fingers digging into the table. The moaning became fiercer, more demanding. I covered my ears but still it was there, assaulting me, calling to me.

There has to be a break soon! There has to!

My throat was so tight I wanted to scream, to tell him to stop, but the music continued fiercer and angrier until again it came to a climax—a gritty, grating noise that set my teeth on edge. Then came a quiet humming. The humming grew and this time again, it was full of pure hope. The melody was stronger now and sounded so free, so joyful. Each note felt like it opened a fresh wound in my chest.

How can someone write music like this? How can he feel that joy?

The musician was bending and swaying with the music, as if the violin was playing him instead of the other way around. The light fell across his face as he rocked backward—his eyes were closed, the music flowing out of him like a waterfall sparkling in the sun. There was such a soaring joy in the music and shine to his face that I rose and staggered down a hall and into a women's bathroom.

My heart was pounding, and the ache in my chest was so horrible I kept gasping for breath. I locked the bathroom door and lurched over to a sink on the far wall. *Am I dying?* I grabbed the edges of the sink and looked in the mirror. My face was white, my eyes dark and alien, and my mouth wide open. It was my mother.

The last twelve years flashed past me as if the mirror were a movie screen, and I saw how I kept turning people away, living in turmoil and fear. Then, frozen in the mirror in front of me, as though he were standing at my back, was Uncle Will, his face wearing the shocked, hurt look it had after I screamed at him about the filly.

My head slumped so under the weight of that, I was unable to hold it up any longer. I felt as if the entire ceiling above was resting on my shoulders, bearing me down to the floor. There was a crush of pain in my chest, and dark spots drifted across my vision.

"Oh, God, what have I done?" I moaned, unable to breathe. "Please forgive me!" A voice resounded in and around me, *My child, I already have!*

The weight was gone with such speed I lost my balance and spun, my back hitting against the wall, and slid to the floor. The ice that held my heart melted, and the years of pain and anger and grief came pouring out.

I don't know how long I sat on the floor, but it felt like an hour. When I stopped crying, I realized that I had been carrying such a burden that it had been weighing me down like an anchor for twelve years. I stood up, my legs shaking, feeling lighter. I was able to breathe again. I looked at myself in the mirror, and a different face stared back. I was changed, not physically, although my eyes and face were red and blotchy. Before they had been cold and pale, but now I could look in the mirror without the guilt that had tormented me for years. Now I could look with a joy mingled with sadness at the areas of my face that reflected my parents' features without wishing that I, too, were dead.

I bent over the sink and splashed cool water on my face and was surprised at how good it felt. I looked at myself again and laughed at the water dripping off my nose. There was a feeling of joy in my heart that I had never felt before. I washed my face again. As I was drying it, I realized that for the first time in twelve years I was happy to be alive. *Music, music, music! It was* music *that broke me loose!*

"Thank you," I whispered.

I came out of the bathroom into the dimness of the poorly lit hallway and began walking toward the main room. The closer I got to the auditorium, the lighter the hallway became. I felt so altered and strange, it seemed I was walking from dark to light. All the lights were back on and the crowd was milling around again, but next to the stage I saw the violinist wiping off his violin. I felt an overwhelming need to talk to him, to thank him. I noticed a dog lying against the wall of the stage, and in my newly born vet's mind, wondered why it was allowed inside. The violinist had finished cleaning his instrument and turned to set it gently in its case.

"Hello. Ian Mackenzie, right?" I asked, and held out my hand.

He finished closing the case before turning. "Yes, that's me." He ignored my hand and didn't look me in the eye. Then it clicked: *he's blind!* I lowered my hand.

"I wanted to say that your music really helped me tonight."

"And your name is?" he asked, now holding out his hand.

"Oh, I'm sorry. Gabrielle Larson. I work with Tracy."

His handclasp was firm, his hand warm. I noticed that his blind eyes were a beautiful gray-blue, unclouded by his inability to see.

"Well, it's nice to meet you. I'm glad you liked the music. Any song in particular?" I felt he could see through me, though he was blind.

"Yes," I said, "the first song you played."

"That's the first time I played it in public," he said, and smiled. "I wasn't sure about it, so I'm glad to hear you liked it." He sat down on the edge of the stage next to his violin.

"Well, I'm glad you played it—it reached my heart." I couldn't believe I was admitting this to a total stranger, but my inhibitions had vanished.

"I'm glad," Ian said.

"How were you able to write it?" I asked.

"Would you like to hear the story behind it?"

"If I'm not being too impertinent."

Ian smiled. "Nice word. No, not at all." He tilted his head toward me and his hair shifted over his forehead. He lifted a hand to brush it back in place, and I noticed his hand and forehead were freckled.

"Then I would love to hear it," I said, and sat next to him on the stage.

"As I said, the song tells a story of part of my life. I'm blind, but I wasn't born that way. I was raised on a ranch, and I was involved in rodeo all through high school. My best friend and I qualified for the high school rodeo finals in team roping. This would have been twelve years ago."

I gripped the edge of the stage.

"Do you know how team roping works?" he asked.

"One rider ropes the head of a steer," I said, "and the other ropes the heels, then they stretch the steer out."

"Right. Well, my friend was the header, I was the heeler. So we get to the finals and are ready to make our run. We get set, the steer comes out of the chute, and bam! We're after him." He slapped his hands together to emphasize the speed, his top hand coasting off his other, following the steer's path in his mind. "My friend ropes the head, but before he can pull the steer to the side, it ducks in front of me and trips my horse. I was thrown off and landed on my head and neck. I was in a coma for two weeks and was blind when I woke up.

"I was blessed not to have brain damage, but I couldn't see that at the time," he said, and laughed. "Literally and figuratively. I recovered from the coma with no other ill effects, but I wished for a long time that I was dead. So I sat in the dark and moped. Finally, my grandpa came to see me one day. 'Ian,' he said, 'you think you have it bad. What about William Wallace? He was Scottish like me, and he had more problems than you!' My grandpa was a boy when his parents came to America—he never lost his brogue or his love and admiration for all things Scottish, including that indomitable spirit. He was ashamed of my weakness, and let me know pure plain what he thought."

Ian paused a moment, then smiled. "He was a good man, Grandpa, and his way of helping was by reminding me of his hero." Ian broke into a brogue, "'William Wallace struggled an' died tryin' tae free an entire nation frae slavery. Yer shamin' yer heritage! All ye have tae do is stop feeling sorry for yerself and do something what's useful!' Grandpa was angry, and he got through to me. I realized I was wasting my life. I was thankful to be alive, and that's when I really started playing the violin. I had played some fiddle before, but that was about it. And here I am, twelve years later. I've learned that even though I live in the dark, I live to seek the light." He smiled and added, "So I'm glad my story and song can make a difference to somebody else."

"More than you know," I said. "Thank you again."

"You're welcome. Well, I should be heading home. It was nice meeting and talking to you."

"I hope I haven't kept you."

"No, not at all. Nope. I hope we'll meet again. Come, Shadow!" His dog, a German Shepherd, jumped up and trotted to his side. Ian picked up his violin and the dog guided him outside. I made my way toward the door, too, and met Tracy there.

"Thank you so much for inviting me," I said, and hugged her. I saw surprise in her eyes when I released her.

"Are you all right?" she asked.

"I'm better than I've been in a long time," I said, and smiled at her. "See you on Monday, right?"

"Right," she said, for once at a loss for words.

I felt light and free as I went home. That heavy lowering ceiling had lifted from my shoulders and flown away.

Chapter
13

I woke up the next morning feeling terrible, and I knew what I had to do. I called the vet's office and asked for a week off. I was allowed time off, but hadn't, until now, thought of taking it. They were able to spare me, so I started making arrangements. I packed a bag and got on a plane to Chicago, the city I hadn't seen in twelve years.

Outside O'Hare, I ordered a taxi to the proper cemetery. There I found a single large headstone for my parents.

> *Daniel and Katherine Larson*
> *"I know that my Redeemer lives."*
> *Job 19:25*

I knelt down and laid the roses that had filled the taxi with sweet scent in front of the stone.

"I'm sorry it took me so long to come back," I said, whispering through my tight throat. "I blamed God, blamed you, blamed myself when you died, and I couldn't forgive. I finally let go, and now it—it hurts *so much!*" I couldn't hold back the tears and felt bent down toward the ground, like an elderly woman, with grief. I dropped into the grass and sobbed until my head ached and I felt dried up.

As I lay there, shuddering with every breath, I heard my father's voice and sensed an arm around me. "Gabrielle, do you know how much we love you?" I laid my head on his shoulder. My mother was there as well, brushing the hair back from my face, smiling as only a proud mother can.

I gasped and sat up. A few more tears slid down my face as I smiled. "Thank you, thank you, God," I whispered.

The evening sun reddened the leaves that hung over me. Night was falling, and I still had a stop to make. I got out my cell and called another taxi. After I tipped the driver and stepped out in front of the house that held the address of my last card, I felt a sudden twinge of nervousness. *What if she hates me after all those cold, polite responses to her letters? You'd deserve that, Gabrielle!*

I rang the doorbell. I heard footsteps approaching the door and had the impulse to turn and run. The door opened.

There she was, older now, but so much the same. "Hello?" she said, then her eyes widened with shock and joy. "*Gabrielle!*"

"It's me, Carmen!" I said, and we hugged each other.

She pulled back to arm's length. "I can't believe it's really you! And you look so good!" She hugged me again.

"You look wonderful, too."

"Come in, come in and sit down and tell me *everything!*" She grabbed me by the hand and pulled me inside.

We talked late into the night, me telling my story, and Carmen telling me about her husband, who was away on business, and showing me their new baby. She was as exuberant as ever, but tempered now with the patience that comes with not living for oneself. She insisted I stay the night with her.

I didn't want to leave in the morning, but I couldn't miss my scheduled flight. We promised to keep in touch and visit again soon, and I intended to keep the promise this time around.

I was tired when I got back to Jamestown, but I made plans to leave the next morning to see Uncle Will and Aunt Bea. I got into bed after making sure everything was in order for an early start.

I woke at one o'clock in the morning, unable to wait any longer. I felt compelled to leave, so I carried my bags into the still darkness and drove off in the night. I could see the eastern sky lightening in my rearview mirror as I drove westward. The dark, star-filled sky in front of me changed to pink-gray as the sun neared the eastern horizon behind.

It was light enough to see fog rising from the ground when I got to the road that led to the Chamberlain ranch. I turned onto the gravel road, driving through the shifting fog that swished aside at my car. I reached the top of the hill before the ranch, stopped the car, and got out. The sun had risen but was obscured by fog. I stood in a radiant canopy of gray and white that shifted around me like tentacles in a dream. The fog was breaking into patches and a few green hills were visible, showing through like sleek fur under a horse's rough, shedding winter coat. The landscape looked old and shrouded in mystery, yet fresh and clean as if reborn.

I closed my eyes and inhaled. I'll never smell anything like that again—the vibrant smell of grass covered with a damp, mysterious chill of fog—the clean smell of growth and life. I felt filled and nourished from breathing the air.

I opened my eyes and saw the fog lifting. The sun appeared through the mist and clouds like a golden swan rising from misty water, its rays like feathers of heaven brushing the earth with blessing.

I wasted so much time because I didn't realize there was mercy and healing waiting for me all along. Why did I think I could make it on my own?

I felt an inner calm. I wasn't alone.

I pulled into the yard, and Oliver walked out to meet me but didn't bark. He was old. I stepped out of the car. It was still early enough for me to wonder if anyone was awake.

"Hey, Ollie." I cradled his head in my hands. "Is anybody up?"

He licked my face and I scratched his ears with trembling hands. I was nervous. I knocked on the front door. Aunt Bea opened it a minute later, still in her bathrobe. I was surprised at the gray in her hair.

"Gabrielle!" Her eyes brightened and she moved to hug me. I held up my hand.

"I have something to say, and if I don't say it right away I might lose my nerve," I said, and took a deep breath.

"Okay, honey, go ahead."

Aunt Bea wrapped her arms around herself, pulling her bathrobe tighter.

"I don't know where to start," I said, "so I'll just say it. I hope you can forgive me for the way I've treated you since you took me in. I've been rude, selfish, unloving, angry, and—" I couldn't go on. "I'm so sorry," I said, and started crying, sending a hand up under one eye like a dam to hold a flood.

"Oh, darling!" Aunt Bea pulled me inside, across the threshold, and embraced me. "Of course I forgive you," she said, brushing my hair back from my face. "I know how hard it's been for you since your mom and dad died. I'm just grateful we were able to do as good as we did by you, because, look, here you are!"

She stepped back and held my face in her hands, smiling.

"You look so good, honey!" She sniffed and wiped at her eyes. "Now, you go see Will. He's in the barn. I'll make some coffee. And breakfast? Hmm? Maybe some muffins."

I smiled and went outside, wiping my eyes on my sleeve. I walked to the barn, dreading seeing Uncle Will because I could still see the look in his eyes from that day, now eight years ago. I paused at the barn door.

It won't get easier.

I went in and stood inside the door, waiting for my eyes to adjust, inhaling the smell I remembered well—the spice of hay mixed with the salt of horse sweat. I saw Uncle Will, leaning against a stall and looking inside, his cowboy hat tipped back on his head. I started toward him, and he straightened at my rustling steps.

"Gabrielle?"

I continued until I was an arm's length away. His mustache and the hair at his temples was gray, and there were deeper lines around his giving eyes. I feared his eyes, how they could cut me with their kindness.

"I've been talking to Aunt Bea," I said, gesturing toward the house. "She said you'd be out here and—I mean, I want to say—" I was out of breath. I stared down at my feet. Uncle Will was silent. I could feel him waiting. My chin started quivering, and I bit my lip and raised my eyes.

"I want to say that I hope you can forgive my selfishness. You taught me so much, and instead of being grateful, I threw it back in your face." I swallowed, trying to loosen the gagging catch in my throat. "I've missed years because of my foolish pride. And you never judged me, you were always kind. I'm sorry!"

I covered my face with my hands and tears seeped through my fingers. Uncle Will drew my hands away, and I was shocked to see his eyes running tears.

"Gabrielle," he said, "from the moment we brought you here, you became the child we always wanted but never had. I only hoped to ease your pain somehow."

I stared at him for a moment, too surprised to speak. "I love you, Uncle Will."

He hugged me and I clung to his jacket, absorbing his warmth and strength, a load lifted from me. He cleared his throat and freed a hand to wipe his face. I smiled at him through a sparkle of tears. When he smiled, his eyes looked like the summer sky after a cloudburst.

He shifted to face the stall again, but kept his arm over my shoulder. "I have something to show you."

I looked in the stall. Inside was a bay mare, a deep bronze-red, with a crooked blaze ending just above her nostrils. It was Anita, the filly he gave me eight years ago. She wasn't tall, but had a slick coat, full muscles, and a sturdy frame.

"She's beautiful!"

"Well, she's still yours, her and the three colts she raised. She's fully trained and a great horse."

I was astonished that he had done this for me, considering the way I treated him. I pulled on his arm until he stooped so I could kiss his cheek.

"You are *still* too good to me!"

He flushed and turned back to the stall and gave a sharp whistle. The straw rustled and a colt untangled his gangly legs, rose out of the straw, and trotted over to Anita's side. I hadn't seen him because he was the same color as the straw. He was a dun, gold with black mane and tail, legs, and dorsal stripe, and wide, dark eyes.

"He looks like a fawn," I said.

"Yep. And you can already tell he's right smart. Friendly, too."

The colt approached us on his long, bony legs, ears turned forward curiously, straw still clinging to his mane. He sniffed my outstretched hand, and then licked it before turning and walking back to Anita. We watched them for a while, and then Uncle Will said, "There's something else I think you should see, Gabrielle. Come with me." He led me out of the barn, his arm still over my shoulder, and led me to a smaller building, one that had always been locked as far as I knew. Uncle Will used a key to unlock a padlock on it.

He turned to me before opening it up. "I know we should have reminded you of this a long time ago, but the time never seemed right somehow. I think it is now." He looked at me a moment, then swung the door open. I stepped into the dark interior and saw neat stacks of boxes and other household items.

"This is most of your parents' personal belongings, Gabrielle. We didn't know what to do with it all, and we didn't want to burden you with this after—" His voice faded as I stood in silence, unmoving. "I'll leave you to look around," he said.

The kindness in his voice held me where I stood until I heard his footsteps fade away toward the barn.

I remained still until my eyes grew accustomed to the semidarkness. There was one window, in the east, and early-morning sunlight was streaming through, illuminating dust motes like sparkling stars. The sun lit some of the cardboard boxes with such intensity they looked ready to burst into flame. I stepped farther into the shed, brushing my hand over the dust on the nearest box.

They had labels in Aunt Bea's handwriting. I stopped at one that read MUSIC. I lifted the box and set it on the concrete floor and knelt beside it. My hands trembled as I pulled open the flaps. It was full of records my parents had collected, along with cassette tapes of their favorite music. The record on top had Beethoven on its cover, and tears blurred my eyes. I remembered a playful argument my parents had over Beethoven.

"My goodness, Kate! That man's face is sour enough to curdle milk!"

"Oh, don't be ridiculous! What he looks like doesn't have any bearing on the quality of his music."

"I'm not so sure. I think Beethoven was so homely he had to be a good musician!"

Why didn't I pay more attention to my parents while they were alive? I thought, and brushed my hand over Beethoven's petulant scowl.

I looked around again. "How can this be all that's left of two people, boxed up and left in a shed?" Even as I spoke, I remembered how my dad once comforted my mom when she was frustrated with the lackluster reception they received at a singing event.

"*You know, it doesn't really matter what people think of us. What matters is what God thinks of us.*"

"*It's still frustrating.*"

"*Dude, look at it this way. We also have a nicely packaged memento of our lives who can tell everybody how awesome we are!*" He grinned in my direction.

"*Daniel, really!*" Mom said, but she smiled at me too.

I wiped at my eyes with a damp sleeve. I looked through a few more boxes, and some of the contents made me laugh. After a while I felt exhausted and wanted to sit in the kitchen with Aunt Bea and Uncle Will, surrounded by the bitter, wholesome smell of coffee. I closed the shed and walked to the house, carrying Dad's Bible and Mom's Beethoven vinyl .78.

Later that day I sat at Aunt Bea's piano. It had been a long time since I played. I ran my fingers over the keys, not daring to press any of them. Finally, I clenched my hands, released them, and began playing "Ashoken Farewell" with faltering fingers. The haunting melody was one of my mother's favorites, and suddenly her presence swept in behind me. The hair on my neck rose, my fingers stiffened. I closed my eyes, and there was my mother, smiling in the way that made her eyes shine.

"*That's beautiful, Gabrielle!*" I heard her say, her voice echoing through the long hallway of all those years. I knew it was a trick of memory, but it was also real. I covered my face with my hands. Arms came around my shoulders from behind—

Mom! No, she never smelled of sterile soap.

"My dear!" Aunt Bea said, "she will always live in your memory. Katherine was a wonderful person, and you are so much like her at times."

"I've been selfish," I said. "I never thought how hard it must have been for you to lose your sister. I was so involved with my own problems I couldn't see anyone else's. I'm sorry."

Aunt Bea looked surprised. "Yes, it was hard. But the fact that we were able to take you in helped immensely. I never thought you were selfish, I only wished there was some way I could have helped you more." She sighed and wiped at a tear. "But, you know, everything has turned out okay, considering."

I laid my head on Aunt Bea's shoulder and she smoothed my unruly hair, so like my mother's. I sat up and smiled at her.

"Thank you," I said.

"Of course," she said. "Would you like some tea?"

I nodded.

That night I dreamed of my father for the first time. I was five, and we were in church. I was sitting on his lap and he had his arms around me. His wool jacket scratched my face, but I didn't mind because I was warm. I knew that the pastor was talking, but I was more fascinated by my father's hands than the pastor's words. I played with his fingers until I tired of that, then I leaned back against his chest, warm and drowsy, and when I woke in my bedroom at Aunt Bea and Uncle Will's house I had a feeling of wool-prickle on my cheek.

Chapter
14

I spent the rest of the week at Crescent ranch, which now felt like home to me. Uncle Will, Aunt Bea, and I would talk late into the night, and I felt I was getting to know them for the first time.

"Did you know that I was in Chicago when you were born?" Aunt Bea asked.

"No, I didn't!"

"Katherine asked me to come out for a visit. So I was there when you were born."

"And Uncle Will was here making hay, I suppose," I said.

He laughed. "I believe I was. I should have been there." He looked at Aunt Bea, not at me, and she sat with her head bowed over her hands, folded on the tabletop. It was the first time I'd ever seen her with every motion of her body stilled, sunk in silence. A growing sadness emanated from her.

I was relieved when she spoke. "It was great that I could be there. But it showed me in an inescapable way what I was missing." She looked at me. "We always wanted children, you see, but it never happened. And here I saw my younger sister with a new baby."

Uncle Will reached out and covered her clenched hands with one of his.

"I had no idea," I said.

Aunt Bea's eyes brightened a little. "It's true that God works in mysterious ways. After the tragedy with your parents, God was still able to bring some good out of the situation, for all involved."

"Yes, he did," I said, and knelt beside Aunt Bea and put my arms around her.

I went for a ride every day I was at the ranch, sometimes with Uncle Will, sometimes alone. I even rode Anita for a while, her colt trailing along. Her gaits flowed smooth as water, with an underlying current of power and speed. She was small and quick, and handled with ease, a sure candidate for a cutting horse, or at the least, an excellent herd-gatherer.

Tears rose to my eyes when I stood brushing her down after the ride. I still didn't believe she was mine. And it was hard to believe what I'd said to Uncle Will—hurtful words I could never take back. Their poison still raged in my head, and I could see Uncle Will's face as my words registered, the shock and hurt in his eyes. I sighed and rested my head on Anita's back. She bent her neck and nuzzled me.

"How could I have been so stupid?" I asked. Her ears tipped forward as if she were considering the question.

"I know what I did was cruel," I said. "Especially after all he's done for me. I hope he really forgives me."

"Of course I forgive you," Uncle Will said from behind. He stood at the stall door, arms resting on the edge, hands hanging down. His smile lit his eyes, even in the dim of the barn. He stepped into the stall and leaned against its side.

"I knew you were in pain, Gabrielle, and I wanted to take that away from you. I saw the joy that came when I said she was yours"—he tipped his head at Anita—"but when I saw the struggle start in your eyes, I knew I'd done something wrong. So I'm sorry if I hurt you, because it's the last thing I wanted to do."

A tear slid down my nose and dropped off the tip as I stared at Anita's hooves. *All you do anymore is cry.*

"You didn't hurt me," I said, smiling through blurred eyes. "I think I was afraid. I didn't want to be hurt again by losing someone

I cared about. I didn't want to love anyone again. So I tried to shut you out. And it almost worked, for a few years anyway. But I was miserable without even knowing it, and I'm sure you and Aunt Bea were miserable too." I rubbed my hand across my eyes. "I'm sorry for that. How stupid, thoughtless, how *selfish* I've been!"

Uncle Will stepped up to me and put his hands on my shoulders and gave me a gentle shake.

"Gabrielle, you were hurt, you were scared, and you didn't know how to handle it. And I didn't know how to help you. You had to go through something horrible. It was hard. The last thing I wanted was to become like my father and grandfather and alienate a person I loved."

I stared up at him, seeing the years-old pain in his eyes. "Uncle Will, it was nothing *you* did. I shut myself up. Don't blame yourself, please. That would make my stupidity harder to bear!"

"You're right," he said, and shuddered, like a horse shaking off flies. "I'm not my father."

There was a moment of silence, emphasized by Anita shifting her weight and chewing on her hay.

"I'm glad," Uncle Will said, "that you seem to have worked through that difficulty. That's what's important."

I smiled again, remembering Ian's hair, flaming under the spotlight, his violin music soaring around me, releasing me.

"Yes," I said. "At least, I've started to."

I spent several days going through my parents' boxed belongings in the shed. I found items I had forgotten about and others I didn't remember at all. One was a photograph of Dad with his family. It must have been taken before he left law school, became a Christian, and met Mom. His whole family looked happy. There was no indication of the stubborn pride that would later tear them apart.

Looking at the photograph, I remembered the day of my parents' funeral, when Dad's mom had sent flowers. *Flowers!*

None of them had come. I was so angry I wanted to rip the photo into tiny pieces and burn them.

How could they not come? They were his parents—his father, his mother! His brothers and sisters! What kind of people are they? How could they let their son and brother be buried and not even show any respect? Didn't they care at all? Did they hate him that much? Hate can work two ways!

My hands shook and I dropped the photograph and stepped to the doorway of the shed. I leaned against the doorjamb, closed my eyes, clenched my fists, and held my breath until the anger subsided enough for me to exhale without screaming.

"Gabrielle? Are you all right?"

I opened my eyes to see Uncle Will on horseback not ten feet away. I had been so angry I hadn't heard him ride up.

"Yes, I'm fine. Well, sort of." I stepped back into the shed and picked up the photograph. "I found this."

Uncle Will clucked to his horse and it stepped forward. He leaned down and took the photo from me. "Your dad's family?"

"Yes."

"Why should that upset you? I've never seen you look so angry."

"Uncle Will, they didn't even come to the funeral. What kind of people don't even come to their son's funeral?"

He looked down at the photo again. "He had a lot of brothers and sisters, didn't he?"

"And not one of them came. Despicable." I kicked the doorjamb. "I hope I never see any of them."

"Well, then, that's what you should do." Gratitude flooded me, until Uncle Will spoke again. "You should go see them."

"You're joking."

"No, Gabrielle, I'm not. I wouldn't joke about such a thing. Take it from someone who knows, you don't want to live with hate like that. It will cripple you."

"I don't understand," I said.

"I know. It took me years to learn." He paused and stared off over my head, squinting against the light from the bright sky. "It might help you if I told you the rest of the story about my dad. You close up the shed and meet me in the barn." He spun his horse around and trotted toward the barn, the picture still in one hand.

I stared after him until he disappeared into the interior of the barn. *I should trust him, he's been right about a lot so far. And I owe it to him.* My shoulders clenched as I turned to close the shed door and follow him to the barn.

The horse he had been riding was haltered and tied in a stall, eating hay.

"Up here, Gabrielle," Uncle Will said, his voice coming from the hayloft.

I climbed the ladder and entered the dim, dusty hayloft. Uncle Will was sitting on a hay bale, leaning forward with his elbows on his knees, looking at the photograph. I walked through the dust-dimmed air, breathing the dry smell of cured grass and alfalfa. The windows at either end of the loft were the only source of light. The barn was so full of life it seemed to breathe—a still, quiet waiting that calmed my anger and soothed me.

I stopped by Uncle Will, and he looked at me. He took off his hat and set it upside down on the hay to his left, and propped the photo inside it. He leaned back against the hay behind him and sighed. I sat next to him and pulled some stray stems from beside me. I waited for Uncle Will to speak, twirling and twisting the stems in my hand.

He ran his hand through his hair. "I'm not proud of what I'm about to tell you," he said. "I know I told you years ago about my dad and mom and that whole situation. Well, the story doesn't end with him leaving, and us staying here. As the years passed, I thought less and less about him. When I did think about him, I got angry. I didn't understand how he could leave me and my mother the way he did.

"Mom and I never talked about him until before she died. She died way too young. I think she was just worn out. There was technically nothing wrong with her, but she started fading away. I was terrified, but I tried not to show it. See, I was only twenty-one.

"One day she asked to talk to me. I didn't know what she wanted, but I was afraid she wanted to make sure I would be all right when she was gone. Nothing could have prepared me for what she did want, though. She wanted me to find my dad. I refused.

"'Will,' she said, 'please do this for me. I haven't asked for much, but I'm asking for this.' I loved her so much and understood how much she'd given up for me that I agreed to look for my dad, even though I hated him.

"I asked her if she had any idea where I should look, so she told me about some of his former friends, and gave me contact information for them. I still didn't want to go. I was afraid she would be gone before I got back. She seemed weak and helpless, and that frightened me because she'd always been strong." Uncle Will clasped his hands together and paused.

"She could sense my apprehension. 'I don't expect you to understand why I'm asking you to do this, Will,' she said. 'At least not now. I'm convinced you will understand some day. But right now it is the task I set for you, so I know you'll do it. And Will, I promise, I'll be here when you get back!' That allowed me to leave—she was one who kept her promises.

"Grandpa and I had a fight before I left that September. He wanted me to stay and finish the haying before going off on such a fool's errand. I told him he should let me go right away because I'd helped him every day I'd been here. He was terrified I was like my father and would never come back. He was too proud to admit that, and I was too stupid to see it." Uncle Will paused again. I stopped twirling my grass-stems and looked at him. He was staring out the far window of the barn loft. His hands trembled.

"Back then you couldn't just do a computer search for a person, you had to hunt them down. So I searched without results for a while. I kept in touch with Mom the whole time, and she sounded cheerful and strong. That enabled me to keep looking. I found him finally, and he was much closer than I expected. He was in a hospital in Minneapolis, in worse condition than Mom. His body was giving out. His doctor said it was from years of living under bad conditions, drinking too much, and not taking care of himself. Add years of guilt to that, and you've got a lethal dose. It was certainly not what I'd expected.

"I'd imagined so many times what I'd do if I saw him. All of that went away when I stepped into his hospital room and saw his wasted body, all the power and danger, the charisma I remembered so clearly—well, it was burned clean out of him. He opened his eyes and stared at me. That was when I finally accepted this man as my father. There's no forgetting the power in those eyes.

"I thought he didn't recognize me because he was silent for a while. Then his eyes filled with tears. 'Why have you come, Will?' he said. 'Have you come to haunt me? To mock me when I'm dying? I might deserve it, but isn't that cruel?'

"I couldn't answer. I wanted to hate him, but instead I felt pity.

"'Well, speak, illusion,' Dad said, 'or go back wherever you came from! Have you come to glory in my suffering?'

"'I came because Mom asked me to,' I said.

"His eyes went hard. 'Does she want all the details of my sad, pathetic life? They're not worth knowing!'

"'I honestly don't know why she wanted me to find you,' I said. 'She's not well.'

"He turned his head away and closed his eyes. 'Margaret, not you, too!' he whispered, and then turned back to me. 'Please, Will, don't leave me!' His voice was pitiful.

"'I'm not leaving,' I said. I almost added *That's your style*, but the thought left a bitter taste in my mouth. I stepped forward and sat in a chair by his bed.

"He looked me over and smiled. 'I think you look more like your grandfather than me.'

"I wouldn't look at him. 'He's been good to me,' I said. 'Taught me a lot.'

"'Yes, you look like Dad, but you remind me of, of Margaret.'

"'That's the best thing you could say to me,' I said.

"The shine of his sick eyes blurred with moisture. 'I know, son, I know you hate me, and rightfully so. But don't forget, there are two sides to every story. Oh, none of that matters now! What's done is done, can't be undone. I'm paying for my actions. Is there forgiveness for a man like me?' His hand twitched, and I knew he wanted to reach out and touch me, or have me take his hand, but we were both proud and ornery.

"'Even a day ago, I would have said that I could never forgive you,' I told him. 'Why didn't you come back?' I reached out at last and took his hand. 'I think everybody would have welcomed you, Dad.'

"He grasped my hand with a feeble fraction of his former grip, and the tears in his eyes spilled. 'I was afraid of that,' he said. 'I didn't deserve that welcome. Every day I ask myself why I left. Every day I ask myself why I never went back. I was never happy there, true, but I belonged with my family. But I couldn't come back and face you all, knowing exactly that—you would forgive me! You were better off without me!' He tried to pull his hand away, but I wouldn't let go.

"'Dad, we should've been the ones to decide that.'

"'I know,' he whispered. 'I couldn't come back because I

couldn't—I can't forgive myself. This slow death, I deserve every minute of it. It's my purgatory. Maybe *God* will forgive me.'

"I spent days trying to convince him to come home with me, but he refused, up to his end. I was there when he died. I think I hastened his death. He was glad to see me, but I reminded him of everything he missed. About his last words were to tell my mother that he loved her and thought of her every day, and wished with his last breath he'd never left—it was her memory that kept him going as long as he had. I was more affected by his death than I thought possible. I realized I'd hated my father all those years because I still loved him.

"I made sure he was buried as he asked, and then I left for home. By now it was early November. I hadn't called over the time I spent with Dad because he'd begged me not to tell Mom I'd found him. Now that I was headed home, so late in the year, I decided not to get in touch first. You had to use phone booths then. No cells. My idea was not a good one." Uncle Will paused and swallowed several times. He leaned forward, resting his elbows on his knees.

"Grandma ran out of the house when I got back, and collapsed on me. 'Why haven't you called!' she cried. My mother was worse. She hadn't spoken for days, and seemed in a sort of coma. But that wasn't exactly why Grandma was so hysterical. Two days earlier, when Grandpa was out feeding the cattle he had a heart attack. Grandma had found him, but he'd been out in the cold for quite a while. Both my mom and my grandpa were in the hospital, and the prognosis, as the doctors say, for both, well, it was bad.

"I was half in shock from Dad's death, so it didn't sink in. I went to the hospital with Grandma, and when I saw them both, in adjoining rooms, the gravity of the situation hit. I sat in the waiting room, shaking. I couldn't go back in either of their rooms. How could I face them? I had left when they needed me the most. I'd done exactly what my father couldn't forgive himself for!

Chapter 14

"Finally, Grandma came and found me. She said that Grandpa was awake and wanted to talk to me. So I went.

"'You came back!' he said.

"'Of course I came back, Grandpa,' I said. 'This is my home.'

"'Yes,' he said. 'Your home.' He closed his eyes. 'Love you, boy.' He was silent after that. He never asked about Dad and I never told him. It looked like he was asleep, so I left and went to see Mom. She was still in a coma-like state.

"I sat in her room for a full day. I knew she was dying and I couldn't bear it. I knew that people sometimes talk before they die, and I wanted to be there if she did. And she did. She woke up as if she'd been napping.

"'Will,' she said, knowing I was there.

"'Yes, Mom?' I bent over and held her hands.

"'He's dead, isn't he?'

"'Grandpa's still alive and kicking, Mom.'

"'No, Will. Your father. He's dead, isn't he?'

"'How did you know?'

"'For all his faults, he could be a good man. Aren't you glad I made you go?'

"'No! I had to leave you!'

"'I know, it was a sacrifice for me. But I had you for years and he only had you for days. I had to make you go, don't you see?' I wondered if she was feverish, but she seemed strong and sure.

"'You knew this would happen? You knew he was dying?'

"'I sensed it. I wasn't sure. I didn't want you to suffer your whole life knowing your dad had died alone and you'd never seen him again.'

"'What if I hadn't seen you again?'

"'I promised, didn't I?'

"We were both silent a spell, but I knew I had to tell her what Dad asked me to. I just didn't know how. My hate for him had returned when I saw all that happened in my absence. Before I hardly thought that, she said 'What did he say, Will? Tell me.'

"I told her what he'd said about how he'd always loved her, and how her memory kept him going.

"'I wish I could have told him the same thing,' she said, with such a smile I realized how much she cared for him and had suffered without him.

"'Mom, how much did you give up for me?'

"'It was for me, too. I couldn't stand moving any longer. I knew if we didn't stay at the ranch we'd be doomed to be nomads as long as we lived.' Mom's voice seemed to be fading, and I wanted to ask her to stop talking. 'I realized that if I didn't tell John that we had to have a real home or we weren't leaving the ranch, then we'd never have a real home. It was the hardest thing I've done. I wanted to believe your dad would stay. But I knew he wouldn't. I couldn't bear to see you uprooted again. Especially since you had learned to love the ranch. It was the first home you'd had, and you are the kind that needs real roots. My heart was torn in two the day your dad left, but I don't regret it.'

"She seemed so frail I clutched her hands in terror. She opened her eyes, and they were younger and plain beautiful.

"'You've grown into a wonderful man, Will. I know some great purpose lies ahead for you. I've been blessed to have such a child.' As her voice got drier and fainter, her eyes glowed with even more joy.

"'Always remember, hate can kill you long before you're dead and guilt will eat you alive. Trust God, he'll take care of you. Will. Peace!' Those were her last words."

Uncle Will's voice trembled and he inhaled. I wanted to hug him, but I could tell he'd thought so long about this story he needed to finish.

"Both Mom and Grandpa died that day. I was full of hate and guilt—no matter my mom's dying words warned me against both. I hated, even cursed, my dead father for taking me away from her when she was sick. And from my grandfather, who had cared enough to raise me.

"For two years I lived with that guilt and anger. Sometime during the third, I felt my spirit fighting back. I began to feel like myself again. Then my grandmother slipped away. Now I felt guilty because I hadn't been there when her husband needed help. She'd never been the same after his death. I felt my whole life was a failure at best, and a curse to others at worst.

"This went on for some years, until the fifth-year anniversary of my mom's and my grandpa's dying. There was a bad winter storm that year. I stood by the window of the house and stared out at this awful salty blizzard. I could barely see the barn. I could hardly bear my existence that day, so I got dressed and went out into the storm, down into the pasture behind the barn.

"I wanted to die, Gabrielle. I wanted all the misery to end. I was bitter and alone. I kept walking, even though it was deathly cold and I couldn't see where I was going. I fell into a shallow ravine and knocked my breath out. I lay in the snow, not wanting to breathe again, but my body reacted and started breathing anyway. Then I remembered my mom's last word. Peace.

"I lay in the swirling snow, empty at last. The hate and guilt were gone. I knew God had driven me out, and that he wanted me to live in peace. Wanted me to *live*. So I went back inside, though I'm not sure how I found the way, and lived. Soon after, I met a talkative young veterinarian named Beatrice, with bright Norwegian eyes." For the first time since he started talking, Uncle Will smiled.

"Eventually, my life made sense again. I went from being bitter and alone to being saved and blessed with a wife, and her eager nature strengthened me. But when I think about those wasted years, I get angry again. At myself. Mom was right. Anger can kill and guilt can eat you alive. Don't give in to them, dear girl."

Uncle Will didn't look at me. Instead he reached down and picked up the photograph. "Find them, Gabrielle. Find them and make your peace with them. If they don't want to have anything to do with you, at least you've done your part. And you never know what good can come of it. Find them, Gabrielle, before it's too late." He dropped the photo back into his hat.

"Tell me, Gabrielle, was I wrong not to tell you my story sooner? Would it have helped with your own grief? I wanted to tell you, but it never seemed right."

He turned to me, his eyes full of a sadness I couldn't bear. "Should I have told you sooner? Could I have spared you years of pain?"

I slid closer to him and rested my head on his shoulder. "Uncle Will, I was so closed off to everyone and everything, I would have rejected your story. Don't blame yourself. I had to come to my own realization in my own way."

I could feel Uncle Will breathing as I spoke. I'd never seen him so emotional before. He looked shrunken, sunk into a pain trying to pull him down.

"You did help me," I said, closing my eyes to see this clearly. "I think if you'd tried to talk to me, I would have lost the part of my life I was comfortable with. I loved your silence. It didn't seem like silence. I could tell you were always thinking, and that was comforting. I felt you could sense how I felt and sympathize without words. That's what I needed most."

I grasped his right hand, and he clutched at mine like it was a lifeline. I opened my eyes after a few moments. The sun had begun its descent into the west, and the rays were low enough that they came with late-afternoon clarity into the loft. The hay-dust looked like incense smoke graying the sunbeams. Uncle Will's left hand was illuminated, his tanned, work-scarred hand resting on his knee. The sunlight sent a shot of gold straight up from his wedding band. I stared at that until the light shifted.

"What is it, Gabrielle?" he asked.

God help me, how can I put it in words? "I feel that I've been blessed, even through tragedy. Who knows what will happen and why it does? I've been given not only one, but two fathers and two mothers."

I looked into his eyes as they warmed from shock into a recognition of the truth of what I said.

"Bless you, child," he said, and kissed my forehead.

I smiled, his mustache tickling my forehead. "Well," I said, "we better go in and see my second mother before she wonders, like, if we've been, like, abducted by Martians or something like that, you know, and *stuff.*"

Uncle Will laughed as I hadn't heard him laugh in a long time. He reached for his hat and held it out so I could take the picture.

"I'll see if I can contact this family of smilers," I said.

"I know."

Chapter
15

I went into Watford City one day, to see how things looked after years away. I had forgotten how everything seemed to rest on either an incline or decline, since Watford City was cut into the hills. Even the main street wasn't level the whole length. The entire town looked different, more open, to me, and there were definitely some new buildings and more traffic. Even so, I figured the change I saw was more in me than the town.

I was walking down Main Street when I heard a voice. "Hey, kid!" I heard someone call, in a voice that sounded familiar. "Gabrielle!"

I turned around and saw Duncan walking toward me in his high-school sauntering walk.

"Whatcha doin' in our neck of the woods, kid?" he asked.

"Duncan, hey! I'm visiting my folks. How are you doing these days?"

"I'm doing *good*. What about you? How has life in the fast lane been treatin' ya? Haven't seen ya around here for years."

"I went on to grad school after college, and I'm working at a vet clinic in Jamestown now."

"Like your aunt. Good for you!"

"Are you still butting heads with your dad over ranching ideas?"

Duncan laughed and scuffed his boot-toes on the sidewalk. "Nah, he came over to my side after seeing my ideas were way better." He grinned. "It took him a few years to get the point, but he came around in the end."

"Well," I said, "that's what matters, right?"

"That's right. But he seemed to listen a little better once I got a family of my own."

"Really? Who's the lucky girl?"

"Well shoot, here she comes now," Duncan said.

I looked where he was pointing and saw my former classmate Kim, leading two young children who held her hands. "Kim!" I said.

She looked up from them and smiled. "Well, Gabrielle, I didn't expect to see you again!"

"I'm sure you didn't. I haven't been here for quite a while. But I was back for a visit and thought I'd come out and see what things looked like. Are these two beautiful children yours?"

Kim smiled wider. "Yes, they are. Davy is five and Joyce is two."

"Yeah," Duncan said, "Kim goes around telling everybody they're mine. Shoot, I don't mind. They're even kinda cute!" He picked Joyce up and cradled her against his chest.

"Honestly, Duncan," Kim said, "I don't know why you say things like that. Davy already acts like you, and Joyce is fearless around horses. It's scary."

Duncan looked at the girl holding on to his jacket. "You're my little horse-girl, ain't you?"

"And I'm your horse-boy, Daddy," Davy said.

"Yes, you are, son," Duncan said as he picked up Davy with his other arm.

I wanted to tell Duncan I remembered his kindness to me when I felt like an alien, but didn't know how to say it. I also wasn't sure he would want to be told.

"It's wonderful to see both of you again," I said, "and have a chance to meet your lovely children."

Duncan smiled. "Good to see you too, kid."

"Yes," Kim said. "I hope it won't be as long next time around!"

"I'm sure it won't," I said.

Chapter
16

I had improved since the confrontation with my image in the ladies room, but there were days that were worse than before. My hard exterior was peeled away and I felt raw. The world looked brighter and sharper, and my senses felt wounded by the end of a day. It made me feel new and weak. I welcomed loneliness before, but now I saw how people interacted with others, a feat I was afraid to begin by initiating contact.

I was walking home after work one evening, in a lovely, crisp hour at sunset. I walked quickly, enjoying the fresh air, and stopped for a minute to watch the pink and gold rising through the clouds from the sliver of sun still above the horizon. A young couple drew near—his arm was around her back, holding her close, and hers was around his waist. They were oblivious to their surroundings, turned toward each other with shining faces, intent on a conversation. He bumped into me as they went past, and then turned, apologized, and turned back to her at once, as if words not used for her were wasted. I walked away, the street dimmed by the darkening sky.

As I wandered through my apartment that night, restless and unhappy, I found the copy of *The Odyssey* Uncle Will gave me as a gift when I left for college. The book was dusty and unread. I had forgotten that Uncle Will gave it to me. I pulled the book out and began to read, and enjoyed the story.

I grew fond of Odysseus and hoped he would reach his much-longed-for home. When he did and found it overrun with worthless young suitors who never had to work a day in their lives, I felt it was one too many burdens for Odysseus to bear. But he did bear it, even gave the young men a chance to leave, but they mocked him. So they all died in agony, slain by Odysseus, his son, and a few loyal servants. I found the poetry captivating and the plot moving and, well, *disturbing* at times.

Why, I thought, *did Uncle Will give me this book when I left for school? Because it's the story of a journey?*

I called him to ask. Aunt Bea answered the phone, so we talked a while, then I asked to talk to Uncle Will. We had talked so little over the phone it was strange to hear his voice contained in an earpiece.

"Uncle Will, I wanted to thank you now, because I know I didn't before, for giving me *The Odyssey*. I admit, to my shame, that I've just now read it."

"Better late than never."

"I guess so. But I feel bad, because it's such a good book. I even forgot I had it! Anyway, I wanted to ask you a question."

"Okay."

"Why did you give me that particular book?"

There was silence on the other end. "Well," Uncle Will finally said, "it is a journey book, and you were heading off to college, which is a type of journey. But I mostly gave you that book because I knew you were upset with me and I wanted to someway show you that no matter what happened or how many years went by, we would still be waiting when you wanted to come home."

"I don't know what to say."

"There's no need to say anything."

"I feel like I've never truly appreciated what you and Aunt Bea have done for me."

"Your life is your appreciation."

"Thanks, Uncle Will, and for everything you've taught me!"

"You're welcome, Gabrielle. But never forget that much of what you know and who you are came from your parents, and they were wonderful people."

"Yes, they were," I said, feeling off balance. "Thank you."

I knew I still needed healing, and one thing that helped me get back on the proper footing was going to church again. I hadn't gone since the days when I went with Uncle Will and Aunt Bea. Tracy recommended a church, and one Sunday I convinced myself to go.

I wasn't apprehensive because I thought the service was going to be bad, but for some reason it was hard to shake off my feelings from years ago, when I felt that the people in Uncle Will and Aunt Bea's church were meddlesome.

I slipped into the church just before the service began. There was an usher standing at the back and he handed me a bulletin.

"Good morning!" he said. "Welcome!"

I thanked him and sat down as the service started.

I don't remember much of the service because I felt awkward and couldn't concentrate. My awkwardness faded after the service was over. Many of the church members came up and introduced themselves and welcomed me. They were kind without being intrusive, and I realized my negative feelings had been the residue of a person I left behind.

At the door, the pastor said, "Good morning. I hope you enjoyed the service." He was a tall, intimidating man, and then I saw his eyes, a mellow hazel with flecks of yellow and brown, so kind and full of empathy I felt I could tell him my life story. "I did enjoy it, yes."

"I'm Pastor John Hennings, but please call me John."

"I'm Gabrielle Larson. Nice to meet you."

"Do you live around here, or are you visiting?"

"I live in town, but I haven't attended here before," I said. "I hope to come back, though."

"That would be great!"

"Thank you again," I said, and at last he released my hand, which had been engulfed in his.

Music was my most consistent help, after returning to church. I let its power in my life at last again, and was soothed and healed by it. I purchased a CD player and borrowed music from the local library. The first selection I listened to was a Mozart violin concerto. I'd never listened to much Mozart, and was amazed by the complex themes underlying his buoyant, energetic music. I couldn't get enough of the joy in his music. I listened to everything of his I could find, and discovered his darker *Requiem* was both wrenching and healing.

I tried Vivaldi's *Four Seasons* because I remembered how much Dad enjoyed it. I was frozen in place as the first strains of music seemed to burst from the CD player. I slipped into that moment, so shortly before the accident, when Dad was listening to Vivaldi. The music, which was cheerful, brought forth such a roiling mass of feelings that I slapped the power button on my player. It went silent, and I stared at it for a minute, shaking, before walking away.

I found it was also too painful to listen to Beethoven's music, since his melancholy melodies were haunted by images of my mother. I went back to Mozart almost in despair. I hoped there were other musicians who didn't inspire such a depth of feeling, ones I could listen to and enjoy for their own talent.

As I continued my search, I came across Anton Dvořák's *New World Symphony*, inspired by his visit to America. I was amazed at his ability to combine folksy music with expansive melodies, and could listen to nothing but *New World* for a week. I began to examine my surroundings more than I ever had, and a longing for the rolling plains ran through me like thick blood. I'd been born a city girl, but that blood had long since drained from me, replaced by the earthy blood of the plains I now considered my home.

Then I made a true discovery. I was standing in the music aisle of a store, looking for more Dvořák. I flipped too far through the music and saw "Bob Dylan," and reversed into a memory I didn't even know I had:

"Daniel, how can you listen to Dylan all the time? He has a terrible voice!"

"Kate, Kate, Kate. Don't you hear the passion? He's a true performer, besides being a genius when it comes to lyrics."

"Well, no matter what, I'll always prefer Eric Clapton. So there!"

"Eric Clapton! Doesn't he wish he was Bob Dylan! In fact, without Dylan, he'd probably still be a nobody!"

"All right, honey. You listen to your Dylan and I'll listen to my classical music. And Clapton!"

I felt frozen in time. To free myself, I reached out and picked up the first Bob Dylan CD in the rack, *Saved*. I was struck by the title and bought the album.

The cellophane wrapper squeaked and crinkled as I tried to tear it off the CD with my shaking hands. My apartment was soon filled with Dylan's growling, nasal voice. I realized Dad had been right. I could hear the passion in his voice. Dylan seemed more concerned with expressing how he felt about what he was saying than about making a pretty impression on others. The depth of feeling in his voice was a quality I'd never heard before. The closest I heard anybody come to this was my parents, who believed what they sang.

Bob Dylan must have experienced every word of his songs. How else could he achieve such gripping sorrow at one moment and such joy at another? I became a Bob Dylan fanatic. I listened to his songs with a voracity I could not explain. He contained an essence so appealing I was amazed that more people didn't see it.

What is perhaps ironic, although I didn't see it that way for a while, is that while I couldn't listen to Vivaldi because it brought memories of my father to me, I realized after listening to Dylan that Dad had imitated him—he had even looked a little like a young Dylan. Dad's style of singing was similar to Dylan's, although the timbre of his voice that rang through my memory was lower than Dylan's.

As I listened to more Dylan songs, I realized that some of the seemingly random statements Dad had made were actually Dylan quotes. The day I listened to "Knockin' on Heaven's Door," I realized what Dad had been referring to in the conversation I overheard. I laughed when I remembered his soapy fist knocking on the air as he sang the chorus. Before I knew it, I was crying. I was remembering their last night. *Why did that song occur to him?* I wondered. *Did he have some sort of premonition?* I shuddered and moved on, some thoughts still too sensitive to dwell on.

I loved *Saved*, the first album I picked up, as well as the albums *Shot of Love* and *Slow Train Coming*. I found it ironic that the albums many criticized Dylan for, his gospel albums, were the ones that drew me to him. There was such heart and beauty in those songs that I could scarcely listen to some without sensing a sting of tears. I particularly loved Dylan's song "I Believe in You." He conveyed a lonely otherness I had felt most of my life. Now I could see I wasn't alone. The song confirmed to me the power of sticking to a commitment, even when the world turns away in scorn.

Perhaps my time away from music allowed me to see into the world in another way. I'd deprived myself for long enough. Now music flowed through my life again.

Chapter
17

I stayed late at the clinic one evening to finish up necessary paper-work. I was responsible for closing since I was the last one there. I locked the door and was finishing up at the front desk when I heard a rattle and knock at the door. It occasionally happened that some-body would come by and see one of us inside and try to get us to work in a last-minute job. I sighed and finished writing a sentence before looking up. Leaning against the door was Ian Mackenzie, his face white, and his hair appearing redder than last I saw him. In his arms was his dog. He was turning away as I opened the door.

"Ian, what's wrong? We're supposed to be closed, but can I help?"

He turned back, a look of relief on his face. "I hope so," he said. "It's Shadow, he's been hurt."

"Bring him in. I'll see what I can do." I held the door open, and Ian carried Shadow through. I put my hand on Ian's arm and guided him into one of the examination rooms. "Here, set him on this table."

Ian bent and placed Shadow on the table, straightened up, and smoothed the dog's head with bloodied, shaking hands.

"I'm sorry I bothered you after you were closed, but this is the only vet clinic I know of off-hand. I know Tracy works here, and I was hoping you'd still be open."

"How did you get here?"

"Taxi."

He was petting Shadow's head, and I was about to tell him that it was fine that he came, but he paused and looked toward me. "Do I know you? You knew my name, and your voice is familiar, but you're not Tracy. I can usually place voices, but I'm a little shaken right now."

"You met me at Tracy's engagement party," I said. "I'm the one who came and talked to you afterward, and you told me the story about your song." I pulled on surgical gloves and stepped to the table to examine Shadow.

"Ah, I remember now. We meet again, under less happy circumstances." He ran his hand over Shadow's head, and Shadow licked at his fingers.

"What happened?" I asked, seeing a long gash in Shadow's side. I probed gently, examining it. It was a clean cut, mostly through skin, but toward his shoulder it was deeper, parting the muscle.

"Well, people ask me to play for many occasions, in all sorts of places. I was playing for a worker's appreciation something or other. Anyway, it was in a bar, and some of the people must have spent all day drinking in preparation. A few of them decided to take issue with me." He smiled, looking even whiter now.

"Take issue?" I was clipping hair away from the wound and cleaning it as he talked.

"Apparently they don't get out much. As I was leaving the bar, two or three guys approached me and started ragging on me and calling me gay. To them, I guess playing the violin means you're gay." He paused, rested his elbows on the table a moment, and placed his head in his hands. "What a stupid situation. Anyway, they were drunk and mean. I was trying to walk away to my taxi, but one of them shoved me, and another stuck out his leg and tripped me, and I fell. Shadow went nuts and must have jumped them because I heard yelling and snarling. I guess one of them pulled a knife and cut Shadow because I heard him yelp, and then the guys ran away.

I could tell Shadow was bleeding, so I told the taxi driver to come here."

I paused, staring at him. "That's terrible! How could anyone do something like that?"

"I don't know," he said. "How is he?"

"He'll be fine, but he needs stitches. He might be a little sore for a few days, but he'll be fine." I prepared the stitching material as I spoke.

"Oh, good." Ian sighed.

"Were you hurt?" I asked. "What about your violin?"

"Ah, no! My violin!" Ian slapped his forehead. "I left it in the taxi. I hope he didn't leave. I have to get it."

"Do you need help?" I asked.

"No, thanks, I'm fine." He stepped away from the table, and Shadow sat up and whined.

"Easy, boy," I said, and tried to get him to lie down again. Ian stepped back and reached for Shadow's head. Shadow thrust his nose out and licked Ian's hand.

"It's all right, Shadow. Lie down," Ian said. The dog obeyed, but his eyes were still fixed on Ian's face. "I'll be right back, you stay here with—" He turned his head my way, embarrassed. "I've forgotten your name, I'm afraid."

"Gabrielle Larson," I said.

He turned back to Shadow. "Stay here with Gabrielle, I'll be right back. Stay."

Ian unclasped a folding cane from his belt, snapped it out to its full length and walked out of the room. Shadow whined again, but stayed still.

"That's a good boy," I said. "Now, I'm going to give you a shot so the stitching won't hurt." His eyes moved to me as I spoke, and I could see that he was anxious. "It's all right, this won't hurt much.

And then I'll be able to fix you." I slid the needle in as I spoke, but he didn't move, just turned his eyes away and fixed them on the doorway.

"Good boy," I said, as I stroked his fur, waiting for the anesthesia to take effect.

Ian appeared in the doorway, grasping his violin case. Shadow slapped the table once with his tail and relaxed when he saw Ian. Ian stood beside the table and set his violin down. I could see he was still pale, so I got him a chair. He sat and placed one hand over Shadow's head, letting it rest there. This seemed to comfort them both.

I began stitching. Shadow lay still, only rolling his eyes now and then. When I was done, I gave him a tetanus shot. Then I tried his reflexes and got a faint response.

"We'll have to wait a while until the anesthesia wears off," I said, "so he can walk properly. It shouldn't be too much longer." I peeled off my gloves and turned to Ian.

"Thank you so much. I don't know what I would have done if—" He ran a hand through his hair. He winced when he touched his forehead and drew his hand away, fingertips bloody.

"You're hurt!" I said. "Let me see."

"Must have happened when I fell," he said, dropping his hand to his lap.

I washed my hands and lifted his hair away from his forehead.

"You have a lump and an abrasion here. Nothing bad," I said. "You won't need stitches, anyway."

He laughed, a sound with the mellow warmth of October sunshine. "That's good, I'm not sure I could take it as well as Shadow."

I got a swab and a gauze pad and came back and held his hair out of the way with my left hand.

"This might sting a little," I said. I wiped his forehead with an antiseptic, but he didn't flinch. I noticed his forehead was paler than the rest of his face, the freckles more obvious. I applied a clean gauze pad and taped it in place after I cleaned the cut. I released his hair, and it fell back in place, thick and heavy, covering the bandage.

"There you are," I said, "that should feel better. And I must say, it's nice for a change not having to worry about a patient trying to bite."

Ian smiled and raised his hand to the bandage. "Who says I don't bite?" he said, and we both laughed. As he lowered his hand, it brushed mine, and he grasped it. "Thank you so much for everything."

He looked up, and I was startled by his eyes. I would have sworn he could see, though I knew he was blind. His eyes were a penetrating steely color, almost as if the blindness gave him greater vision than normal eyesight. I blushed and lowered my eyes. Then I felt foolish for blushing because he wouldn't know I was staring.

"No problem," I said. "All in a day's work." I realized he was still holding my hand. "I should check Shadow again," I said, and his fingers gave in release. I checked Shadow's reflexes again and they were nearly normal.

"Hey, big boy, want to try walking?" He looked up at me and sat up. I lifted him off the table, avoiding touching the stitches. He walked, a little stiffly, over to Ian and licked his hands.

"Hey, you," Ian said, "you gave me a scare! Don't do that again, huh?" He held Shadow's head between his hands, and Shadow's tail waved as he licked Ian's nose.

"Do you have a phone I can use?" Ian asked. "I need to call another taxi."

"I'll take you home."

"I don't want to trouble you any more than I already have."

"Nonsense, it's no trouble," I said. "It would be my pleasure. In fact, we could go to my apartment for some coffee or tea, if you like."

That might make you feel better. Did you know the English think sweet tea is good for shock?"

Ian's face brightened. "I did know that. But since I'm Scottish, I could use some coffee instead."

"Well then," I said, "it's settled."

I next saw Ian and Shadow sitting in the waiting room at the vet clinic, Ian with his hand on Shadow's neck, Shadow with his tongue hanging out in pleasure.

"Ian," I said, "and Shadow! How may I help you two?"

Ian stood, and then Shadow. "Gabrielle, hello. I was in the area and thought I'd stop by and show you your handiwork."

I could feel Tracy looking at us as I knelt beside Shadow. "He has healed well," I said, running my fingers across the scabbed cut. It was clean and dry.

"Yes, he's as frisky as ever, thanks to you. I'm very grateful. I don't know what I'd do without him."

"He's a great dog," I said. "And how about you? No scars, no concussion?"

"Nope. See?" He lifted his hair away from his forehead.

"Ah, so I see," I said. "Very good."

"I was also wondering if I could return your favor."

"What favor?"

"Take you somewhere for coffee sometime."

"I see, *that* favor. Well, sure, why not?"

Is this really you, Gabrielle, talking to someone this easily?

"Excellent!" He smiled, as if an ordeal was over. "When would be good for you?" he asked. "I'm free almost any time this week."

"How about tomorrow, after I get off work? Is around five okay?"

"Works for me," he said, and smiled. "I'll meet you here."

"All right."

"I better let you get back to work so they don't lock you in again.

Come, Shadow!" He turned back toward me at the door, "Until tomorrow then," he said, and was gone.

I laid my clipboard on the desk and tried to ignore Tracy's smile, but then she giggled. I tried to give her a cold stare, but smiled instead.

"*Sooo*," she said, "is that a date?" Her eyes were large, questioning, but she was trying to keep a straight face.

"Just coffee."

"Mm-hmm," she said, and looked out the door. Ian was walking down the sidewalk on the other side of the street, Shadow at his side.

"You know," Tracy said, "they say that the way to a man's heart is through his stomach, but for Ian I think it's through his dog."

We watched them walk away, Shadow's tail waving as he walked.

"You're probably right."

I realized, after we met for coffee, that I felt comfortable with Ian, as though we'd been friends for a long time. We started meeting regularly. Tracy teased me, acting as if she had set us up. Ian and I were merely friends, I told her, and she gave me a coy look and nodded in a knowing manner. I let it go—I figured she wanted to set me up with somebody because she wasn't single any longer.

In spite of Tracy's teasing about double dating, I suggested the four of us go out sometime. Ian had been friends with both Tracy and her fiancé, Jason, for years. I ended up regretting the suggestion.

Ian and I met Tracy and Jason at a coffee shop. Tracy was cheerful and pleasant, as usual, but Jason was different from the times I'd been around him before.

"Hey, Ian," Jason said, "how're ya doing, old buddy?" I sensed a forced heartiness in his manner.

"Hello, Jason," Ian said, "I've been doing well. How about you?"

"It's good to see you, Ian," Tracy said. "It's been a while."

Jason treated Ian as if he were injured and needed special attention. Tracy noticed this and tried to compensate by acting normal, but she overdid it and became studied and stilted in all she said and did.

Ian remained kind and asked questions about their lives that would soon be united. If he noticed their behavior, which I was sure he did, he made no allusion to it. I was saddened that people who had been friends of his since before he was blinded could treat him differently than they had before. It seemed callous not to meet him where he was. Ian didn't make an issue of his blindness, and I didn't see why his friends should.

He was silent for a while as I drove him home, and then he said, "It's nice spending time with friends."

I didn't know how to respond. *Surely he noticed how they were treating him?*

"You were rather quiet."

"I was listening to you all talk," I said, not wanting to tell him how I really felt. "I didn't want to intrude on the conversation. You've all known each other so long."

"That doesn't matter. You're a friend, too."

"I'll keep that in mind."

"I'll hold you to that!"

I was glad to see that he wasn't bothered, at least not that I could tell, by Jason's behavior and Tracy's overcompensation.

"Well, here we are," I said.

"Thanks for the ride. And for arranging the get-together. We need to do that more often. Life changed a lot after my accident, and some things are still different. But friends are friends, no matter what." That was his only allusion.

One afternoon when Ian and I were having coffee, I realized I was still grieving over the loss of my parents. Ian sat stirring the foam on his latte. He didn't realize that some of it was stuck to his thumb. I was going to tell him, but he was in the middle of a funny story. At one point, he rubbed his thumb across his eyebrow, leaving a trail of white. I stopped laughing. Ian's hand had turned to Dad's, rubbing soap-foam on himself. I could see the scene in such vivid detail that Ian faded out of my sight.

"Gabrielle?" I heard Ian's voice as if from a distance. He reached out and found my arm. "Are you okay?" he asked.

"Yes, I'm sorry."

"Did my story offend you?"

"What? Oh, no."

"What, then?"

"It was something you did." I was still trying to shake the grasp of the past.

"What?" he said.

"It's okay, it's not something you did so much as something you reminded me of. A long time ago, my parents were having a serious conversation, and I overheard part of it. They thought I was in my room doing my homework but I was in the hallway listening to them talk as they were doing the dishes." I was barely making sense to myself, so I paused to gather my thoughts into coherence.

"What did I remind you of?" Ian asked.

"Well, at one point my dad accidentally rubbed soap foam on his eyebrow," I said, and saw Ian's confused expression. "You didn't notice, but you rubbed milk foam on your eyebrow. It reminded me of them."

Ian laughed, rubbing both eyebrows with a napkin. My eyes filled with tears, and Ian must have sensed that I was not laughing with him. "Sorry," he said. "I didn't mean to be insensitive."

"I miss them," was all I could get out.

Ian reached across the table, palm up, and I put my hand in his.

"I'm sorry, Gabrielle," he said and squeezed my hand. "Is there anything I can do?"

"Nothing that you haven't already done," I said. "Sometimes it helps to talk about them."

"Any time you need to talk, I'm here."

"I know. Thank you."

Chapter
18

$\mathcal{T}$he first time I set foot in a bar, I went to hear Ian play with a local band on an open mike night. He'd mentioned it in passing but hadn't made a point of saying I should come, so I decided to appear as a surprise. I was the one surprised.

The band was performing country and bluegrass music, with Ian playing a "mean fiddle," as the lead singer called it. Ian was wearing jeans, boots, and a cowboy hat. He looked more natural in that attire than the rest of the band, reminding me that he had once been involved in rodeo. The bass guitarist had ripped the sleeves off his button-down plaid shirt, so his T-shirt sleeves stuck out through the armholes.

Ian's foot tapped to the beat as he played, and he drew some lovely, sweet fiddle-music out of his violin. The real surprise came when he stepped up to the mike.

"We're going to do a song a few of you might know," he said. And he began sing-talking a song I'd never heard before. "The devil went down to Georgia, he was lookin' for a soul to steal." The audience burst into whistles, slapping tables and stomping their feet. Apparently it was a popular song. I was too amazed to applaud. *Ian sings?*

And then he broke into the wild, crazy fiddling that I found out the song was famous for. Still, at the chorus, when the other singers joined in, Ian's voice rose above the rest with an expansiveness I could not describe.

I applauded and whistled along with the rest of the crowd at the end of the song. Ian raised his hat and smiled. "Thank you! Thank you all! And thanks to Mr. Charlie Daniels!" The crowd whooped again.

I pushed up to the stage as the musicians were packing their instruments.

"Ian, I didn't know you could sing!"

"Gabrielle! I didn't know you frequented bars," he said, grinning under his hat brim.

"To be honest, this is the first time I've been in one."

"Really? Well, maybe we should celebrate that with a drink. I'd have a drink, but you know me, little lady, I never drink and drive!" He winked.

"Well, neither do I, so that rules me out, too. Sorry!"

"Aw, that's okay. But hey, I'm glad you came! Did you like the music?"

"Yes. I didn't realize you were so diverse. I forgot you said you originally played fiddle music."

"Yeah, sometimes I feel strange if I don't play it for a while. And it's fun playing with a band."

"Do you write your own songs? I know you compose music, but do you write lyrics as well?"

"I haven't, really, up to this point. I've been thinking about it recently. I think I'd like to try." He picked up his violin. "I should learn to play the guitar or the piano. They would be easier to use when working on lyrics."

"If you need help with something, I can play the piano a little. Of course, I don't *have* a piano!"

"Thanks for the offer, I'll keep it in mind. You wanna get out of here? I can only take the noise for so long."

"That makes two of us."

"When I was younger, my friends called me Granny because I couldn't stand loud music."

"Well, I didn't listen to music for years. And I guess the loudest noise I was around was the baler when my uncle and I made hay."

"Ah, making hay. Good times. That sweet smell!"

"I miss haying with my uncle." I hadn't realized until then that was true.

"Well," Ian said, as we went outside into the clear night air, "I don't want to keep a working girl like you out late on a weeknight." He laughed and turned his head, as if to get his bearings.

"Does a fiddling man like you need a ride home?"

"Ma'am, I couldn't possibly trouble you after you already took time out of your busy schedule to hear my band," he said with a cowboy drawl, and tipped his hat.

"Yes, like, interrupt my *terribly* busy social schedule," I said in my best valley-girl voice. "It's no trouble. I have to drive home anyway, so I might as well drop you off on the way."

"If you insist, it would be rude to resist. Hey, I got the rhyming thing down. Maybe I am ready to write some lyrics!"

The next evening, Ian called me and said, "Gabrielle, were you serious about helping me with song lyrics and music?"

"Sure. I don't know how I'll help, but I'll do what I can."

"Excellent! I'm scheduled to do a concert at Jamestown College in two weeks and it would be good to have some new songs. If possible. So any help would be appreciated. Maybe I can give you 5 percent of my stipend!"

"I'll do what I can."

"Okay, great! So, another favor. Are you free right now? And if you are, could you pick me up? The college people told me I could use their practice rooms if I wanted, in the fine arts building, so I thought maybe we could go up there and see if the anticipated inspiration strikes."

"It sounds like it has. I can pick you up in about ten minutes, if that works."

"Ten minutes it is."

Ian was waiting outside his apartment, and we drove up to the college, to that campus so familiar to me, although I felt strange being there. I parked in front of the fine arts building, and inside we found an empty practice room with an upright piano against one wall.

"Okay, so I've been working on something, but I can't seem to get it to come out right. It's kind of a silly song, but, hey, I wrote it!" He began humming, a sound that reverberated in the small room, and soon I could make out the words he was singing.

> *There once was a young man, Henry by name.*
> *He was wild and free, drowning his shame—*
> *And lived a hard life, no one to blame.*
> *Henry was a writer, he spoke in rhyme—*
> *Wrote out words in metered time—*
> *Images spun, he never made a dime.*
> > *Wouldn't you know it?*
> > *Haven't you heard?*
> > *Penniless poet,*
> > *Writing his words.*
> *Others listened as he spoke his thought*
> *But turned away, he was not what they sought.*
> *Henry's words began to fester and rot.*
> *Yet still he spoke where no one would dwell*
> *He was alone in a dark wordy hell—*
> *He turned to words he knew he could sell.*
> > *Wouldn't you know it?*
> > *Haven't you heard?*
> > *Penniless poet,*
> > *Selling his words.*

Now Henry wrote heavy words about fate—
Had followers who thought he was great—
He felt imprisoned by those words of hate.
Henry kept writing and singing his songs
But now he felt dull, hollow, and wrong—
Felt that all the good words were gone.
    Wouldn't you know it?
    Haven't you heard?
    Penniless poet,
    Singing his words.
Then came the day when Henry was broken—
His heart dried up, his eyes were a-smokin'
Dark were the words by him then spoken.
And then he heard a voice from on high,
"Stop selling your words and you won't go dry,
Always be truthful and you'll cease to die."
So Henry left his dark, dismal way
And stepped into the light of day.
With words purer now he began to pray.
    Wouldn't you know it?
    Haven't you heard?
    Penniless poet,
    Healed by words.

Ian's singing faded back into humming, his voice still ringing in my ears.

"Ian, that's not silly. I like it!"

"Something's still not right, and I'm not sure what. It's frustrating!" He ran both hands through his hair, and I smiled at the way tufts stuck up on his head.

"I did notice something . . . sticky? In the chorus?"

"Exactly. But I don't know how to fix it." He began humming the melody for the chorus again.

I hummed a simpler, countermelody, and he stopped.

"That's it," he said. "Do that again!"

I hummed the simpler version again, and Ian picked up the melody and began singing the chorus: "'Wouldn't you know it? Haven't you heard? Penniless poet, Healed by words.' Yes, that's better! Thanks! Now I *will* have to give you a percentage!" He leaned toward me. "How did you know it should be simpler?"

"Dad always said the most beautiful music is often unbelievably simple."

"Well, he was right. Can you play the melody on the piano?"

"I can try."

I was able to pick out the melody after some trial and error, and Ian began singing. It was a simple melody, but it complemented the words, and when he got to the chorus, I began singing harmony without realizing what I was doing.

"Gabrielle!"

"What?" I stopped playing, my hands trembling on the keyboard.

"You have to sing this song with me!"

"Me? No, I can't!"

"Why not?"

"I just can't."

"It won't be the same without you. Couldn't you please try? At least practice it with me, then if you really feel you can't do it for the concert, you don't have to." He reached out and touched my arm. "*Please*, Gabrielle?"

My hands slipped off the keyboard and rested in my lap. "I haven't really sung since my parents—"

I brought my elbows down on the keyboard in an atonal crash and rested my head in my hands. Ian moved in and sat next to me on the piano bench. "I'm sorry, Gabrielle. Of course you don't have to sing. I just thought the song would sound better. But don't feel pressured to do it if you don't want to."

His voice was gentle, comforting. I inhaled, shaking. "Okay, I'll practice with you. But I'm not promising anything. Even the thought of singing—"

"I know. But maybe it would be good for you to do this. Like I said, I'm not trying to pressure you, I just want you to think about it. But if it upsets you, you don't even have to practice it. Okay?"

He ran his hand through his hair again, and I could see red-blond hairs rise on his forearm. He smiled, and I saw that his eyes had a multidimensional pattern of blues and grays raying out from the perfect black circle of his pupil.

"Shall we practice then?" I asked.

"Lead on, maestro!"

I realized how terrified I was when the day of the concert came. I wanted to tell Ian I couldn't sing with him, but that would be pathetic after all our practice.

The concert was slated for the college chapel, so we were in the basement, preparing to go on, or rather I was pacing back and forth through the cool basement as Ian tuned his violin and warmed up.

"Gabrielle, you're not nervous are you?" he asked, as I walked past him for maybe the tenth time.

"Why?"

"I may not be able to see, but I can hear you wearing a path in the concrete. And I can feel nervous waves washing around. And they aren't coming from me! Or not much anyway. I get nervous to an extent, every time I perform. But I always remind myself I'm not performing for my own glory or reputation."

"My parents told me the same thing," I said, and sat down near him.

He lowered his violin from his chin. "You'll be fine, Gabrielle. I know it's been a long time since you sang in public, but just imagine we're still practicing."

"I'll try."

He smiled, raised his violin, and ran through a two-octave scale.

I clenched my shaking hands in my lap. I would have to play the piano with these on Ian's last song, the one I was singing with him. My fingers were sweaty and trembling, and I wasn't so confident I would be able to play.

"Okay," Ian said, "it's time!"

We went upstairs to the main floor. We entered the sanctuary area, led by the head of the Jamestown College music department, who introduced Ian while I sat in one of the front pews, trying to remove from my mind the sight of the nearly-full chapel.

I got caught up in Ian's music. He played a variety of styles of violin—fiddle, folk, classical, his own compositions. I was amazed again by his skill and ability to connect with the audience. I tried to ignore the glints of light shining off the piano I would have to sit at and play soon.

The song Ian chose before his new composition was a quiet, meditative piece. I bowed my head and closed my eyes and heard my father's voice say, as he did before every performance, "*God, help us and give us strength to do this for you.*"

The song was over. Ian waited until the applause faded, then said, "The last song of the evening is a new type of song for me, so I hope you'll bear with me. I wrote a song with words. It's my first, so you should hold off on the tomatoes this time."

I laughed along with the audience, and some of my nervousness faded.

"To aid me in this new endeavor, I recruited the help of one of my friends. Please welcome Gabrielle Larson."

Polite applause rose from the audience as I walked to the piano. Ian tilted his head in my direction, waiting until he could hear me settle myself on the piano bench.

I began the introduction when he nodded. He held his violin

and bow in his left hand and the microphone in his right. He began singing and his baritone filled the chapel, resonating through the open space.

I was playing mechanically, until we got to the chorus. When I began to harmonize with Ian, my nervousness faded. I could hear the blend of our voices, and it reminded me of my parents and how they loved to sing. My voice could never be mistaken for my mother's clear, bright soprano or Ian's baritone for my father's voice. But the act of singing with someone brought tears to my eyes.

My voice didn't choke up as tears gathered in my eyes. I even closed my eyes, and continued to play the right notes. I was filled with strength and talent not my own. I played on until the musical bridge before the last section. Ian played that on the violin, bringing a resolution to the song before we rounded it out with the last verse and chorus.

While he played the bridge, I was filled with a joy so powerful that I stayed on the bench only by grasping its edges. I wiped away my tears and felt as if the joy must be leaking out of my skin with enough luminescence to light the chapel.

We finished the song, and the audience rose to their feet, applauding. I saw Tracy standing with a surprised look on her face. She came over to me as other audience members went to talk to Ian.

"Gabrielle," she said, "why didn't you tell me you were singing? Ian told me about the concert and to come for the surprise ending. Boy, what a surprise! I didn't know you played the piano or sang! You were both amazing. Why didn't you tell me?"

When I could get a word in, I said, "I'm sorry. I was so nervous, I didn't think to tell anyone. And I never told anyone that I could sing or play because—well, I'm over that now. Thanks for coming! It's nice to see somebody I know!"

She lunged forward and hugged me. "You were great. Ian better watch out, or you'll take all his business! You could be the singing vet, and do concerts for animals!"

I pictured dogs and cats listening, ears cocked, some cows in the back chewing their cuds, and laughed.

"That's okay," I said. "I think I'll keep my day job."

"That's good," Ian said, joining our conversation. "I don't want you to put me out of business. If you do, I'll haunt you so much you'll have to put me to sleep!"

"You're the real musician. I wouldn't worry about it!"

"Deal! I can never eat much before a concert, so are either of you ladies interested in getting food somewhere?"

"Sure!" Tracy said.

"I don't think I ate today," I said, "so I could be persuaded."

"Food, here we come!"

As we sat in the restaurant together, my feeling of joy didn't fade, and as I was driving Ian home, I said, "Thank you for encouraging me to sing with you tonight. I can't explain it, but it was somehow healing for me."

"Well, I'm glad. And you sounded wonderful. I might have to bring you along more often!"

"I don't know about that!"

"Gabrielle, the song wouldn't have been the same without you."

Chapter
19

$\mathcal{I}$ drove to Ian's place to pick him up for a coffee outing, pulled up and parked, and walked to the door, inhaling the fresh air. I heard Shadow bark once as I knocked, and Ian called to me to come in. Shadow came to meet me, wagging his tail, and I saw Ian in the living room, sitting on a couch, a book on his lap.

"Gabrielle, in here," he said. Shadow led the way into the living room and lay down by Ian. The book on Ian's lap was in Braille, and his finger was stopped on one spot. His face looked clouded, somehow distant.

"What are you reading?" I asked.

"Have you ever heard of the poet Gerard Manley Hopkins?"

"Um, a long time ago. Mom used to recite one of his poems, something about the grandeur of God and the wings of the Holy Spirit, I think."

"Mmm," he said. "Well, I'm trying to read some of his poems, but I seem to have forgotten his cadences. That's important, since the sound of his poems communicated his thoughts and feelings." He sighed. "My grandfather used to read them to me, but the echoes have died because I can't seem to hear them right when I read them to myself."

He looked right at me, and I flinched and averted my eyes. *Why does it sometimes seem he can see?*

"I kept my grandfather's copy of Hopkins. I don't know why, but I still have it. Do you think you could find it and read me a poem or two?"

"Of course," I said, though I was reluctant.

"It should be over there on the bookshelf." He pointed with unnerving precision. I located the book—the cover was worn, the binding loose, and some pages were dog-eared and had marked lines. The pages themselves were smooth and gray with age and smelled of old paper and tobacco.

"This book has seen some use," I said.

"Grandpa carried it with him a lot. He must have admired Hopkins if he forgave him for being one of the vacillating Irish."

"Which poem would you like to hear?"

"Well, I was trying to read 'The Windhover,' so I'd like to hear that one if you can find it."

I cleared my throat and turned the worn pages until I found it. Its page was dog-eared, with minute writing in the margin. I began reading, conscious of how my voice sounded.

"'The Windhover: To Christ Our Lord,'" I said, and paused.

> I caught this morning morning's minion, king-
> dom of daylight's dauphin, dapple-dawn-drawn Falcon, in his
> riding
> Of the rolling level underneath him steady air . . .

My voice increased in volume as I worked my way through Hopkins's words and got caught up in his energy. I seemed to gain the rhythms and timbre of my mother's voice in recitation.

> . . . sheer plod makes plough down sillion
> Shine, and blue-bleak embers, ah my dear,
> Fall, gall themselves, and gash gold-vermillion.

The last words rolled out of me, driven by the poem. The printed words quivered on the page in an absolute silence.

I glanced up from the book and into a moment removed from

reality. Ian was sitting with his eyes wide open, staring into a beam of sunlight that illuminated his hair in its own flame of gold-vermillion, and a tear slid out of one steel-gray eye and down his face. I shivered, as if Hopkins's ghost was in the room. Ian sighed and closed his eyes. The moment was gone.

"You're still standing," Ian said. It wasn't a question.

I went across the room and sat next to him, still silent.

"You read well." He reached up and wiped his eye, and I wanted to hug him, but a distancing sadness spread from him like another self.

"I remembered how my mom recited that poem, and the cadence seemed to come on its own."

He smiled at me. "I'd say so. It confirmed what I suspected—Hopkins was meant to be read aloud or heard, not read silently." He turned his hands palm-up, and I could see faint Braille indentations on his fingers.

"Gabrielle, may I ask you something?"

"Of course," I said, but a dread-like thrill went through me. He was serious, more so than I'd ever seen him.

"Are you—" His fingers curled onto his palms, and he turned his hands, now fists, back over. His knuckles gleamed white through his pale skin.

"You're not friends with me because I'm blind, are you? You know, because you're sorry for me, because you want to *help* me?"

"Of course not!" I said, and grasped his hands with mine. He flinched, not expecting my touch, then clutched my hands. His were cold.

"Ian, I'm your friend because I want to be your friend, because you're a wonderful person. In fact, I feel you've helped me more than I'd ever be able to help you! Any small thing I could do can't compare to what you've done for me, and anyway, friends are supposed to help each other."

"So I'm not a complete waste of oxygen, then?"

"Don't be stupid!" I said. I leaned forward and hugged him. I felt awkward because both warmth and a tension I hadn't expected flowed from him. I sat back. He laughed, but I couldn't tell if the sparkle in his eyes was from mirth or tears.

"I've been a wee daft laddie todae."

"No more Hopkins for you!" I said. "Next time let's try something lighter, like *Macbeth*. Or anything by Thomas Hardy, or perhaps Emily Dickinson."

"Ah, yes! Let's do that, next time."

"You should never think of yourself as less than you are because you're blind. What about John Milton? He was blind, yet he wrote this little book called *Paradise Lost*. Perhaps you've heard of it? Anyway, you can also see things that supposedly normal people can't. That's a gift, Ian. So is your music."

"I know, Gabrielle, but some days I feel I'd give it all up for one minute of sight. To be able to see a sunset, a tree, a leaf, a face. Then one of my friends reads Hopkins to me!"

"Not again for a long time. It's going to be Shakespeare or nothing next time!"

"Shakespeare, huh?"

"That's right! Mom also loved Shakespeare—she and Dad would literally run around the house pretending to be Beatrice and Benedick or even Kate and Petruccio. Dad would call her his Kate-shrew sometimes. Of course, one of his favorite quotations was, 'Come, kiss me, Kate.' I usually ran off like they had the plague. If only I'd known." I sighed. "I can hardly watch some of the plays."

"It sounds like they were great people."

"Yes," I said. "But now whose turn is it to be down-in-the-mouth!"

"I know!" Ian said, nudging me with his elbow. "We should go. Our coffee is getting cold."

"What coffee?"

"The coffee we are hypothetically going to buy once we arrive at an establishment that sells it."

"Oh right. The *hypothetical* coffee!"

Once Ian realized I was a new-born music fanatic, he recommended CDs for me to listen to, even loaning me some of his favorites. One day he surprised me with a gift. We were out driving around, and he pulled a CD from his pocket.

"Here, for you," he said, and I saw it was still wrapped in cellophane.

"What's this?" The cover had several figures on the front, and in antique-gold letters I saw *The Lord of the Rings: The Fellowship of the Ring.*

"You've never seen the soundtrack for *The Lord of the Rings?*"

"Not that I know of. What is it?"

"What's *Lord of the Rings?*" Ian said. "I thought everyone had seen the movie, even if they hadn't read the books. You've never read the books? Or seen the movie?"

"I've never heard anything about it."

"How is that possible?" he said, and laughed. "We have to remedy this! Of course, I haven't seen the movie either, but I read the books years ago, and then I listened to an amazing BBC audio version. Oh, oh"—his voice dropped to the wistful—"I wish I *could* see the movie."

"So this CD, it's the music from the movie?"

"Yes. The composer should have been knighted for it, even if he's not British! Here, let's listen to it." He took the CD from me, unwrapped it, and handed it to me to put in my player.

The car was soon filled with a rich, ethereal sound that expressed both melancholy yearning and foreboding.

"This is only the music from the first movie. There are two others."

"Oh, why?"

"Well, there are three books, so they made three movies."

"Oh."

The intensity of the music affected me so much, I resisted an urge to pull my car over to the side of the road. Just then, the song switched. The next song began with a mellow flute solo, taken over by bouncy, lilting strings.

"Ah," Ian said. "The hobbits."

"Hobbits?"

"You don't know about hobbits? The little people? This is one of the main songs about them."

"Little people? Like in Irish stories."

"Not exactly. It's hard to explain. Hobbits are also called half-lings. They usually live in houses that are dug into the ground. They like to eat, plant gardens, smoke tobacco, and—You know what? You're just going to have to read about them."

"I guess so," I said.

The music changed again. Now it was dark, pulsing with an ominous beat, chasing, threatening. But, no matter how dark the music got, the main theme rose up, triumphant, like a warrior leaving the battlefield, scarred but victorious.

I had to read the books, I had to see what led to the creation of such music. It was more than epic. It was moving in a way beyond description.

"Ian," I said, "do you have the books?"

"Yes, I do! Well, somewhere."

"Could I borrow them?"

"Of course! In fact, we could go hunt them down right now."

"Okay," I said, and swung around to Ian's apartment.

We found the books after a brief search. They were in a slipcase holding three volumes of the Lord of the Rings trilogy along with *The Hobbit*, the prequel.

The music intensified again, as I was driving home by myself. There was a background of staccato, male chanting, overlaid with brass and strings. The music built and rose until it hit an eerie climax that faded into humming, and then through that cut the pure, tragic voice of a boy, his high voice lifting through the mists of the lower notes of music. I began reading as soon as I got home.

I read the books as quickly as I could. Even *The Hobbit*, which was really a children's book, had an appealing charm about it. But the trilogy held me spellbound. I voraciously went through *The Fellowship of the Ring*, *The Two Towers*, and *The Return of the King*, staying up late reading until I seemed wrapped in a fog, transported to the elder world of Tolkien's creation.

Ian was amused, still amazed that I'd never heard of the books. He was glad I was reading them, and enjoyed discussing them with me.

"Everyone should have a friend like Sam," I said to Ian.

"Yes," he said. "Sam has always been one of my favorite characters. Although I like Faramir as well."

"He's truly noble."

"I've also always admired Èowyn," Ian said. "It takes courage to defy the rules of society, even if you do it for the wrong reasons."

"But think," I said, "if she hadn't disguised herself, wrong or not, how would the battle have ended?"

"Mm hmm, very true. I think Tolkien is showing us that it's not what she does so much as her attitude. She wants to die. That makes her fearless, but it also makes her willing to throw away her life without thinking how it will affect anyone else."

I stared at Ian. His head was tilted slightly, an eager, intent look on his face. I smiled.

"Yes," I said, "there is worth in every life."

Chapter
20

I had delayed my promise to contact Dad's family long enough. I knew I'd never do it if I kept putting it off, and I had to keep my promise to Uncle Will.

I found information about the family law firm, which they now called Larson & Sons, on the Internet. *So Dad's father must have been able to convince some of his sons to become lawyers. They are my grandparents and my uncles and aunts, and I've never once seen them.*

I could feel the tremble of anger beginning at the back of my knees.

"Stop it, Gabrielle, stop it!"

I located their home phone number through the online yellow pages, after confirming where they lived. *Weldon and Mary Larson. And they still live in Chicago. I'm glad I don't live there any longer. Do I really have to call them? Maybe I could write. Gabrielle, call them!*

I set a card with my grandparents' number in big black numerals on my table. It stayed there for days. I picked up the phone one day after work and dialed the number, praying no one was home.

"Hello?"

"Oh. Yes. Is this Mary Larson?"

"Yes. To whom am I speaking?"

"Gabrielle Larson."

There was a strangling, gasping sort of noise on the other end of the line.

"Gabrielle?" she whispered.

"Yes. I wanted to say, that is, I wanted to thank you for the flowers you sent to my parents' funeral. I never thanked you before. I wasn't in a very good frame of mind, well, for years afterward, but I should have thanked you." I didn't know what else to say. I resisted an urge to hang up.

"Gabrielle! How have you been? I wanted to call you so many times, but I didn't know if—I didn't know how to get hold of you."

"I'm sorry, I should have called or contacted you. I've been meaning to for a while, but I didn't know how you'd take it. I know there were hard feelings between you and Dad."

"No, we should have contacted you. But Wel—no, you were a mere child. My, you must be all grown up by now. Where do you live?"

"I'm in North Dakota, working at a vet clinic."

"North Dakota! I think your call was meant to be. Weldon and I will be in Grand Forks in two weeks. I want to come visit you."

It was my turn to make a strangled sort of noise.

"Unless, of course, you'd rather not see us."

I held the phone with both hands, pressing it into my ear, so I wouldn't hang up.

"You should come."

"Thank you."

She gave me the information about the days they'd be in Grand Forks, and I gave her information on how to reach me. Exhaustion poured through me when I hung up the phone, feeling almost too weak to set it in its cradle. I had to put it out of my mind. *Until they get here*, I thought. *I won't think about them until then. I can't.*

Chapter
21

*I*an liked to go for walks, but he told me he enjoyed them more if he wasn't alone, so as often as I could I went with him.

I called him to see if he wanted to go for a walk the day after my call to Mary Larson. I couldn't call her my grandmother. I needed to get out for a while, to clear my head.

We were walking down Main Street, and I saw a couple of men ahead of us, leaning against the side of one of the buildings. They were talking in loud voices.

Ian stopped. "Gabrielle. I recognize one of those voices. That's one of the guys that cut Shadow."

"Are you sure?"

"Yes, I'm sure. I know his voice."

Shadow growled.

"See?" Ian said. "Shadow recognizes him too."

"Okay," I said. "Let's keep going and ignore them."

"Lead on."

We kept walking, and on impulse I grabbed Ian's arm and drew him close. I looked at him with adoring eyes, knowing he couldn't see.

"Oh, honey," I said, too loud, "don't be silly!"

Ian went white, then red, then smiled at me.

I continued saying nothing of importance to him in a sultry voice until we were past the two men—overdressed wannabe cowboys with vinyl boots and shiny straw hats with rolled brims—who were staring at us with wide-open eyes and mouths. I smiled at them, simpering, as we walked past.

I laughed, natural again, and gave Ian's arm a gentle squeeze before letting it go. "You should have seen their faces," I whispered.

"Yeah?" Ian laughed a strange laugh.

"Hey, you didn't have to worry about them. They weren't going to do anything. They're cowards, peckerwoods who've never had to do ranch work, trying to look like cowboys. I thought we should help them reevaluate their prejudices."

"Good for you! I wasn't worried about them. You can't let people like that ruin your day."

"Agreed," I said.

Ian seemed off-kilter and strangely distant for the rest of our walk.

How can people be so foolish and ignorant? I thought. *I hope those men learn a lesson someday. Ian shouldn't have to suffer because they're mean and petty and can't think when they're drunk, the cowards!*

Ian still seemed quieter than usual when we ended our walk in front of his place.

"Are you all right?" I asked.

"Yes, I'm fine."

"Don't think about those guys anymore, they aren't worth your time."

"What? Oh, no, I won't. Have a good evening, Gabrielle."

"You too."

As he walked inside, I wished there was some way I could lift his burden of blindness, some way I could help.

The call I'd been dreading and purposely not thinking about came on a Wednesday. It was my grandmother calling to say she and my grandfather were in the state. She wanted to know if they could come and see me over the weekend.

"We wouldn't take up much of your time," she said. I could tell she wanted to be considerate, but I could hear a longing in her voice.

"That would be fine. I'm afraid you won't be able to stay with me. My apartment is minuscule. And none of the hotels in town are quite on par with what you are used to, I'm sure."

"That's no problem, that's not why we are coming. You're sure this won't be an imposition?"

"I think it's necessary, don't you?"

"Yes. Right. Well. Why don't you expect a call from me some-time on Saturday?"

"I'll talk to you then," I said, and set the phone down and rested my head in my hands.

How can I do this? I'm still so angry at them. God, I need the strength to have mercy! Anger can kill, remember?

I told Ian about my meeting and how much I was dreading it. He offered to go with me, but I felt that would give my grandparents the wrong message, meaning that we were romantically attached, or worse, that I was unwilling to face them alone. He said that if the meeting went bad, I should call him and he'd come to the rescue.

But this is something I have to face on my own. I have to do this.

My mind gnarled in knots of anger and pain as I drove to a cof-fee shop to meet my grandparents.

How can I have never met my grandparents? How could they have done what they did? Maybe they've changed. But better not hope for miracles.

I walked into the coffee shop and knew at sight which woman was my grandmother. She, too, turned right to me. She walked toward me—looking nervous and tentative, her eyes and lips heavy with makeup. Her immaculate, tailored suit made me feel out of place in jeans.

"Gabrielle," she said, and held out her hand. I stared into her hazel eyes, darker than my father's, perhaps darkened by grief and age, and took her hand, ignoring the burn in my stomach.

Can I hate her because she has Dad's eyes?

Her silver hair was short and stylish.

"You have Daniel's eyes," she said. "Weldon will be coming along shortly. He had business calls to make first."

He didn't want to come. Damn! Do I even want to meet this proud, hateful man?

"Well," I said, "we can order coffee while we're waiting."

We sat and talked, Mary mostly asking about my present life. We both avoided discussing our family.

She looked up, over my shoulder, and her eyes darkened. *Fear?*

"Weldon," she said.

I stood and turned to face the enemy. I could see a hard glint glaze over his eyes as I stared at him. I was wrenched and couldn't speak—my father would have looked like this if he had lived long enough. My grandfather stood staring at me.

"Come sit down with us, Weldon," Mary said.

It seemed both an entreaty and a demand. He stepped forward and sat, boom. He unbuttoned his suit jacket and looked around, as if passing judgment on the establishment.

"I don't know why we have to dredge up the past," he said, surprising me with his bluntness. "What's past is past."

"Weldon, please."

"Even the past can be mended," I said. "There's no sense of time in God's outlook."

He stared at me with the shock of seeing a mad woman. "Is that what Daniel told you? After he refused to see us?"

"Dad taught me about mercy, but my Uncle Will taught me forgiveness."

I turned to Mary, who was looking distraught, trying to pull a tissue out of one of those little packages. "There was wrong on both sides of the situation, but we can stop the cycle of suffering."

"Good God," Weldon said. He stood up and walked away to the counter to order coffee.

Mary dabbed at a tear. "I'm afraid I was not entirely honest, Gabrielle," she said. "I made Weldon come. I told him he had to. I'm sorry."

Uncle Will was right, I thought. *They are suffering.*

"I'm glad you made him come, and that you both did. It's time to face all this, but I simply don't know how to."

Mary glanced over at Weldon, who was stirring cream into his coffee.

"He's full of anger," she said. "I was always too weak to stand up to him. Until now. I think that's the only reason he came—he was shocked that I insisted."

He came striding back to our table and sat.

"Grandfather," I said, "tell me what Dad was like when he was young."

He stared at me, shocked. I could see a film like an inner curtain draw over his eyes. He looked down at his coffee.

"What do you want to know?" His voice was louder than necessary.

"What he was like before he went to college. I never got a chance to ask him."

Weldon flinched. "A lot of us never got—Daniel was a lovely child until he went off to college and met a bunch of hippy idiots who filled his head with claptrap—foolish notions!"

"Like being happy with his life?" I asked. "Then marrying a person he loved—maybe having a family—that part, I suppose."

Mary laughed, a nervous spasm. Weldon looked me up and down, his chin thrust out, and then sighed and seemed to shrink inside his stylish suit.

"Maybe you're right," he said. "Maybe it's time to cauterize the past."

"I don't know where to start," I told him.

He stared at the steam rising in curls from his mug, as if he could find the answer, genie-like, in it. Mary twisted and played with the sparkling rings on her fingers.

"I have a question," I said. "Why didn't any of you come to the funeral?"

Mary's hands stilled. "I wanted to come, but, well—"

"Say it, Mary!" Weldon said in a burst. "You didn't go because I wouldn't let you!" There was a tone of scorn in his voice, but he looked stiff and uneasy.

"Why wouldn't you let her come?" I asked.

"Because Daniel told us to stay away from his family," he said, his jutting jaw clenched.

I leaned against the back of my chair. "I didn't know that."

"I don't imagine he would have told you."

"Weldon, there's more to it than that," Mary said, and turned to me. "Yes, Dan did say that. And it hurt. But I don't blame him anymore. He was being pressured constantly by his family, I mean, by *us*." She glanced at Weldon. "Daniel was even told that if he left your mom and you—you were just a baby at the time—that he would be guaranteed a good job working for Weldon. His dad."

She stared down at her rings. "I'd never seen Dan so angry. He said, 'Until you can accept my choices and respect my family, don't bother trying to contact us anymore.' Then he turned to me and said, 'Mom, if you ever want to talk to me about anything other than changing my lifestyle or abandoning my family, I'm always willing to listen.' He walked away. We never should have let him go." Mary's voice caught, and she stopped speaking.

"As if we could have stopped him," Weldon said. "Daniel was

always so proud he wouldn't let anybody change his mind once he'd made it up."

"Where do you think he got that from?" Mary said.

"True, I am a proud man. But I would never walk away from my family."

"But isn't that exactly what you asked him to do?" I said.

Weldon stared at me as if this was a recurring, not altogether pleasant, thought. "Maybe he was more like me than I'd care to admit. Damn, he was a son a man could be proud of! He should have worked with me in the firm. He'd still be alive today."

"Maybe," I said, "but would I be?"

Weldon looked straight at me, but I did not let him stare me down. I wanted him to say what I knew he must be thinking. He'd rather have Daniel alive than me. He sighed and lowered his gaze instead.

Calm down, Gabrielle. Remain calm. God help me, I'm still angry at him! Look at Mary, look at your grandmother. She's suffering too, she's suffered enough. I see Dad's kindness in her, even distorted as it seems through time.

Weldon placed his hands on the table and pushed his chair back, as if he was about to rise. "Well," he said, "I don't see that we're accomplishing anything here."

I reached out and touched his hand, which was cold and dry. "Grandpa, please don't leave."

He slumped back in his chair as if I'd hit him.

"I have ten other grandchildren, and I've never felt that way when they call me Grandpa."

"I have something to say before you go," I said. "My parents, both of them, would want me to learn to love you. And I want to. So what I have to say is, *the past doesn't matter any longer.* I don't harbor any ill will toward you. That's gone."

And as I spoke, the last vestiges of anger and blame melted like snow under a warm rain, as though speaking the words generated their release. "It doesn't matter what happened any longer. It's in the past. But let's not let the past rule our lives. I know it must hurt you every day that Dad walked away and that you never spent time with him again. But I also know that he always thought of you. He kept this."

I pulled the photograph I'd found out of my pocket and placed it on the table.

Mary gasped and snatched it away. "I remember this afternoon!" she cried. She dropped it on the table and covered her face with her hands in the exact way I so often did.

Weldon reached out to pick it up. The tremor in his hands caused the picture to waver.

"We all look so happy," he finally said.

In those simple words I could hear the broken man inside him speak, the one he tried to hide, speaking of the past in the present tense.

Chapter
22

I called Ian the next day and told him I needed to get out, to rid myself of the tension left from my grandparents' visit. It was the first time we had gone for a walk since our encounter with the men who attacked him, and he was cheerful and energetic as usual. We walked over the smooth green grass in one of the city parks, enjoying the sound of the breeze through tree leaves and the ripple of water flowing nearby.

Ian broke away from me at one point and ran down an incline, chased by Shadow, who barked and leaped at Ian's side in warning. I ran to catch up.

"Silly!" I cried. "Why are you running?"

"So you'd run after me!" Ian said, catching me by the arms and spinning me around.

"I think you drank too much coffee or something," I said, dropping to the ground, dizzy.

Ian sat next to me, his face turned my way, his eyes more expressive than any I'd seen.

"Sometimes one just *has* to run!" he said, leaning back on his elbows, inhaling the grass-scented air in a long intake.

"True," I said. "I miss running some days. I ran track in high school."

"Really? You must be a good runner then. You could probably catch me with no problem!" He grinned at me, eyes mischievous.

"Could be." I said. "Although I was more of a distance runner than a sprinter." I looked up at the cloudy sky. "It looks like rain."

"And what does rain look like, pray tell?"

"Okay, smarty, it looks like rain might originate in that sky above and soon descend upon us. Is that better?"

"More accurate, anyway. I can smell rain. And the air has cooled."

"You can?" I asked. "I can't smell it."

"It's been said more than once," Ian said, "that when you lose one sense, you rely on the others to a greater degree. They become enhanced to compensate for the loss."

"Sounds reasonable. But what happens to people who don't have any sense to begin with?"

"They become bureaucrats."

I lay back in the grass and laughed until my stomach hurt. "Oh," I said, "good one!"

Ian closed his eyes and turned his face to the sky, smiling, as the first drops fell. I rose, ready to return to the car, but he didn't move. He lay there, eyes closed, letting the rain darken his hair to rusty-brown. Raindrops slid off his cheeks like tears, yet he smiled.

"I love the smell of rain," he said. "And I love the feel of it on my face. I always have, even when I could see. There's something peaceful about water that arrives from heaven."

Perhaps only a blind man can truly appreciate something as simple as rain, I thought, as a drop rolled from my hairline, and I felt its path sliding down the side of my face.

"Well," Ian said, "I suppose we better go, before Shadow gets so wet he permeates your car with wet-dog smell."

"If that, like, totally bothered me, do you, like, think I'd be a vet?"

Ian sat up and held out a hand, smiling. "Help an old man up?"

"Yes, Grandpa," I said, grasping his hand, and remembered how I'd used that word with Weldon.

He rose, with no real help from me, and I could see a dry spot on the grass in the shape of his body. His hair was dripping water onto his forehead and he brushed his hand across his face at those sweeping pieces of chestnut hair that kept falling over his forehead. "Ah, rain. Unfortunately, it's not exactly a warm rain. Otherwise you would have had to drag me away kicking and screaming."

"Well, I'm not sure I could drag you, so it's good it's not warm."

I was cold and clammy by then, so I turned on the heat in my car as we drove away from the park.

"Describe the color of the sky to me," Ian said.

"What?"

"What does the sky look like? Every time I saw rain the sky looked different in some way. Describe what you see. Please."

"Okay, but don't laugh." I glanced up through the windshield. "Um, the sky is a solid pale gray with clusters of darker gray clouds moving lower to the ground and starting to travel faster. Everything looks gray because the sun is covered and because of the rain. The grayness seems like a waiting—the trees are drooping forward, as if they're contemplating something. You know how rarely there is no wind—because it is still, it looks like a world devoid of hope, living in anticipation. Yet there's something, as you said, peaceful about it. Oh, I don't know what I'm saying!"

"No, that was a good description," he said. "I know what you mean about the gray quality of light. You've got a good eye, Gabrielle."

I didn't know if Ian realized how ironic a statement that was for someone like him to make. My eyes burned, and I rubbed them.

During a particularly tedious day at work, I found myself looking forward to seeing Ian after work. But I went about my business until Tracy stopped me, an incredulous look on her face.

"Gabrielle!" she said, scrutinizing me.

"What? Did I do something wrong?" I looked down at the papers in my hands.

"You're humming. You never do that!" She tapped her nails on the counter and raised her eyebrows. "I think Ian's gotten to you!"

"Oh, don't be silly," I said. "I've told you before, we're just friends."

"Right. That's what I thought about Jason," she said, and awarded me with her believe-it-or-not smile. "But if that's the way you feel, you better be positive that Ian feels the same, because you don't want a mess later on when you realize he's been pursuing you and you wanted only friendship."

She grabbed my arm. "Think about it," she said, "are you positive he just wants to be your friend, and nothing more?"

"Yes, of course I'm sure," I said, but she had planted a seed of doubt. Now I was apprehensive about seeing Ian.

When I met Ian later, he was his usual cheerful self. I studied him, trying to figure out if he was interested in me in any other way than as a friend. I'd never had much experience with this sort of thing because I'd always shut people out. He seemed at ease and calm, not nervous or concerned about impressing me. This satisfied me—he *was* just a friend.

"You're quiet tonight," he said. "Anything wrong?"

"No, nothing's wrong. I was just thinking."

"Ah, thinking. I try that sometimes. I find it very, *very* hard work." His eyes sparkled, and I laughed.

"I know what you mean. Sorry I was quiet."

"That's okay. May I ask what you were thinking about?" He rested his elbow on the table, his chin on his fist. His hair had fallen across one of his eyes, and I wanted to brush it back.

"Oh, nothing important, really," I said, blushing. "Just something Tracy was saying today."

"Ah, Tracy, the talker!" he said with a smile. "I've known Tracy for a long time."

He paused, and his eyes became distant, as if tuned in to a time when he could see. He brushed the hair off his forehead. "I used to go riding with her sometimes," Ian said. "I even had a crush on her before my accident." He paused, his face settled and sad. "I miss those rides."

"Do you still like her?" I asked, thinking, *Lord, I hope not. She's engaged!*

Ian laughed. "No, all that was over a long time ago, even before I became obsessed with my problems. I mostly miss horses in general."

He sighed and ran his hand through his hair, resting his forehead in his palm for a moment. He straightened and smiled. "Anyway, enough ancient history," he said.

I could see the pain in his eyes, and was silent for a moment, trying to capture in words the thoughts that spiraled like quicksilver through my consciousness.

"Have you been around horses at all since your accident?"

Ian's smile was sad. "Not really," he said. "At first by choice. I think I even blamed my poor horse for my blindness. Some of my friends thought it would be good for me to be around horses. They tried their best to get me to cooperate, but I was too sunk in misery to do anything other than lash out at them. After that, they seemed to switch to thinking I should stay away from horses." He sighed. "I just don't know."

I clasped and unclasped my hands several times.

"If you had the chance," I said, "would you want to be near a horse again, maybe even ride one?"

He raised his head, a flush obliterating his freckles. "I think if I could just smell a horse again," he said, "I'd be happy for a long time."

"What are you doing this weekend?"

He frowned. "Nothing, as far as I know. What's the point of all these questions? Thinking of being a CIA vet?"

"Too much lying for my taste. No, I've been wanting to visit my aunt and uncle, so I was wondering if you'd be interested in coming along with me, this weekend or some other time that might be better for you. Uncle Will has lots of horses, wonderful horses."

"I don't know," he said. "I hadn't thought—I don't know." He looked away as if taking in the larger world. "Much as I'd like to be around horses again, I wonder if it would be more harmful or painful than anything." This he said with his head down. "It seems like a dream, that part of my life. Maybe it's better left that way."

"Well, think about it and let me know if you change your mind."

"Would you think me a coward if I didn't want to go?"

"Not at all." I reached across the table and patted his hand. "It's up to you, whatever you're comfortable with." He squeezed my hand and smiled even though he looked wan, pallid—his freckles stood out like miniature jagged puzzle pieces.

"I'll think about it," he said.

The next morning he called me, and I could hear an eagerness in his voice.

"I couldn't sleep last night for thinking, and I decided, if the offer still stands, I'd love to go with you this weekend. If you're still going." He sounded breathless.

"Great!" I said. "I think you'll enjoy it."

We worked out the details, and hung up. I had already told Aunt Bea I would be visiting, but I called to fill her in. She was ecstatic. She loved company.

Chapter
23

*I*an and I left for the Crescent ranch after I got off work on Friday. Ian sat in silence for most of the drive, fidgeting with his hands, touching his hair, and rubbing his knees as though his palms were sweaty. Shadow picked up on his nervousness and would occasionally whine from the backseat.

By the time we got to the ranch, it was ten-thirty, dark and still. We stepped out of my car, and Shadow leaped over to Ian's side. They stood still as I stretched, easing the traveled miles out of my back. I went around the car to guide them to the house, and I saw that Ian's eyes were closed. He breathed so deep that he swayed.

"That smell." His voice sounded reverent.

I could smell the dark pungency of pines and the spice of drying grass, pressed down by the cool, dark night.

"It's wonderful, isn't it?"

"Beautiful, beautiful," he said, almost whispering.

My eyes had adjusted to the dark by now, and I looked up at the sky. "The stars!" I said. "I forget how bright they are out here."

"I can imagine," he said. "Describe them, please."

"I don't think I can," I said.

"Try."

"The sky is so black that it looks soft and the stars look hard. But not really hard, either, but so bright that their light hardens, holding them in the soft sky."

My voice came out sounding strange because my head was tilted back.

"And the Milky Way. It looks close enough to touch tonight—it's like a dust cloud of light, a pathway of angels. That sounds like a cliché. But what I've thought about it is probably sillier. I've never told anyone what I think about the Milky Way. It looks, well, good enough to eat. If I were to eat some of it, the creamy light would be so nourishing I'd never have to eat again, and light would seep from my pores." It was a thought I sometimes felt would restore my parents, or unite me with them, and I could feel the dew of tears gather on my lashes. Ian laughed, but not in derision. It was a warm, happy sound that sounded as clear as the starlight itself.

"Gabrielle, I think you have the soul of a poet."

"We should go inside before my aunt and uncle realize I'm waxing poetic about stars again."

Aunt Bea and Uncle Will welcomed us with their usual warmth, and Ian appeared to feel right at home. He said he was tired after the trip, so I led him to the guest room.

"Do you need anything?" I asked.

"No." He smiled. "I'm fine, thanks."

"Well, if you need anything, just ask."

"I will. Goodnight."

"Goodnight."

I joined Uncle Will and Aunt Bea, and we chatted for a while.

"He seems like a nice young man," Uncle Will said. "How did you meet him?"

I told them the story and explained how Ian had helped release me to the breakthrough I'd had. They listened with interest.

"Yes, I noticed the violin when he came in," Aunt Bea said. "I was wondering about it."

"He doesn't go much of anywhere without it," I said. "I'm sure he'd be delighted to play for you."

I got up early the next morning and went down to the kitchen. Ian was already there, with Shadow at his feet, talking to Uncle Will. Aunt Bea was busy making enough breakfast for ten.

"Good morning, sleepyhead!" Uncle Will said. "Last one up does the chores."

"I'd be happy to, Uncle Will."

"Nah, you're here to visit. You do whatever you want." He took a sip of coffee, his mustache bristling. "I put Anita in one of the stalls. Thought you might want to see her."

"Thank you, I'd love to!"

Uncle Will came over to me as I was putting on my boots after breakfast. Ian was talking to Aunt Bea, thanking her for breakfast.

"Gabrielle," Uncle Will said.

"Yes?" I looked up at him, one boot on, struggling with the other one.

"That's a right nice young man there," he said.

I straightened up, surprised. "Yes, he is," I said. I didn't know exactly where he was going with this, and I wasn't sure I wanted to know.

Uncle Will nodded, patted my shoulder, and turned back into the kitchen. I stood there a moment, still with only one boot on.

I gave Ian my arm to help guide him to the barn, after suggesting that Shadow stay in the house. He was a good guide dog, but he wasn't used to horses.

"Say," Ian said, "you're almost as good as Shadow!"

"Oh, stop it! You better behave, or I'll lead you through manure!"

"Ach, terrible!"

Ian's joking seemed a mask for his nervousness, and when he heard a horse whinny I felt his grip tighten on my arm. I looked at his face—he was so pale his eyes looked more blue than gray, as if his emotions were draining blood.

We entered the barn and walked down the concrete aisle, footsteps echoing in the welcoming space, until we reached Anita's stall. Ian's grip on my arm was so tight I could feel my pulse throbbing under his hand.

"Are you okay?" I asked.

He nodded and licked his lips. I unlatched the door, and we stepped inside the stall. Anita was facing away from us, but she turned her neck so her head was near her shoulder and snorted at us. Her eyes were bright and her ears twitching.

"This is Anita," I said, "the one I told you about."

Ian licked his lips again and swallowed. "Right," he said. He held out his right hand, and Anita placed her nose on it and lipped his hand. Ian reached out with his left hand and felt her face. He felt his way across her head to her neck, then grasped her mane. I could see he was shaking. He stepped up to her, circled her neck with his arms, and buried his face in her mane. Anita's eyes opened wide, and she sniffed Ian's back, then sighed and relaxed, her eyelids drooping. I scratched her blaze and watched Ian.

"She's beautiful," he said, his voice muffled by her black mane. "I forgot how good a horse can smell. Well, no I didn't. It's not something you forget." He raised his face, shining and happy.

"What a good horse. Thank you." I didn't know if he was thanking me or Anita.

"Do you want to ride her?" I asked.

He turned to me, his blind eyes wide.

"Do you think—? Would I be—?"

I could see the hope in his eyes. I put my hand on his arm.

"You can do it," I said.

The joy shone out of his eyes, and his smile grew until it pulled a laugh out of his chest. "All right," he said. "It's not like I can damage myself much more anyway, right?"

He stood with a hand on either side of Anita's head, talking to her, as I saddled her. I led her to the round pen, and guided Ian as well. I explained to him where we were, and he nodded. He had used round pens before. I led him to Anita's side and placed his hand on the stirrup to show him where it was. He was trembling again, his face flushed.

"You can do it," I said, squeezing his arm. "I'm right here."

He took a deep breath, placed his foot in the stirrup, grasped the saddle horn, swung on with cowboy ease, and settled himself in the saddle. Then he looked nervous. I handed him the reins.

"Remember, you're in a round pen, she can't run off on you."

"That's good. Is she prone to running off?" He laughed and settled himself more. He closed his eyes and squeezed Anita's sides with his calves. She stepped forward to the fence, moving along its circumference. Ian sat and let her walk for a while, getting used to the feel of riding again. Occasionally, she would step close enough for his toe to brush the fence, but she always stepped away again. He grew more confident, stopped her, turned her, and went the other way. This continued for a while, until he halted her and patted her neck.

"Gabrielle?"

"I'm right here," I said, walking up to Anita's side and putting my hand on his leg. He sighed. "She handles like a dream," he said. "Maybe I'm dreaming. Do dreams make you greedy? Because I want to gallop!"

He covered my hand with his. "Do you think you could, um, ride in front of me on Anita?"

"If that's what you want."

He didn't have to speak, I could see it in his eyes. I led Anita out of the round pen, and Ian slid back and sat behind the saddle. I adjusted the stirrups and climbed on in front of him.

"You can hang on to me," I said, and he wrapped his arms around my waist. I walked Anita out of the yard, into the winter pasture, open and empty, and out into the tall-growing grass, rustling in the breeze.

"Are you ready, Ian?"

"Never more so," he said. I nudged Anita and she started off in her springy trot. I nudged her again and she began loping in smooth, easy strides.

We loped for a while, until Ian said, "*Faster!*"

I loosened Anita's reins and clucked to her, and she leaped forward, leveling out, racing through the grass. The wind rushed through my hair and my eyes watered. The thrill of our speed brought a smile to my face. Anita ran with her head up, snorting—I could feel the joy of running coursing through her muscles.

I looked over my shoulder to see if Ian was all right. His head was tilted back, his red-brown hair whipped away from his forehead, his eyes closed and his mouth open, so it seemed he was drinking the wind. We went on until we topped a hill, and I slowed Anita to a trot, then a walk. I stopped her and sat looking at the landscape below.

Ian slid off, so I did too. I dropped Anita's reins to the ground, knowing Uncle Will had trained her to stay. Ian stood at her side, facing her, with his hand resting on her rump, head bowed. Anita snorted a few times, then lowered her head and began ripping up grass.

"Gabrielle?" He held out his hand to me.

"Here," I said, taking it in mine. He turned toward me and my heart fluttered in double time before resuming its normal beat. His eyes were full of tears.

"Gabrielle . . . I . . . that's the best thing anybody's done for me."

He paused, and I could see him struggling with emotion. "Thank you," he said, and a tear ran down the side of his face.

I reached up and brushed it away without thinking, and felt my eyes fill, too, with tears. He looked straight into my face, and I flushed. I was sure he could see me. His eyes grew clear again, the color of the sky above—steely gray-blue clouds lit from behind with an undetectable brilliance.

His hair stirred in the breeze and he reached out and touched me with his fingertips, running them over my face. I grew light-headed, realized that I'd been holding my breath, and let it out in a sigh. He smiled and drew me to him.

"Thank you, Gabrielle," he whispered in my hair. "Thank God."

I had shunned human contact for years, and now realized how right it felt to have his arms around me, hearing the beat of his heart as my head rested on his chest. I was speechless, but more than that, I didn't want to talk. He pulled back after a while, but kept his hands on my waist.

"It's your fault, you know," he said, and smiled.

"My fault? What is?"

"I'm going to have to retitle my old song and write a new one." He brushed his hand over my head, smoothing my wind-tossed hair. He must have felt the question I didn't ask.

"It's you, Gabrielle. When I'm around you, I don't care if I'm blind, even though I do wish I could see you. But it's because I'm blind that I met you. And since I met you, you've filled my life with meaning. You are music to my eyes."

"Ian, there are better people, less messed-up people—"

"Gabrielle. Stop." Ian pulled me to him, enwrapping me in the same embrace. "People are worst at judging their own worth. Surely you believe there is a reason you were spared, some reason you're alive?"

I nodded, my cheek scraping against his shirt.

"I don't have the answers," he said, "but I know that I feel more alive than I have in years, maybe ever."

I couldn't speak, but I hugged him back.

"My new song for you," Ian said, "goes something like this." He cleared his throat and began humming. It was a beautiful melody, filled with lilting cascades of notes. I closed my eyes and rested my head on his chest, that heartbeat, his arms still around me.

His song contained the beat of his heart, the gentle swishing hiss of grass around our legs, the grinding crunch of Anita eating grass, and the chirp and flutter of birds flying across the dome of heaven that covered us.

I could hear the clank and rattle of falling chains.

Reading Group Questions

1. There are many themes in *Past Darkness*. Which one did you resonate with the most?

2. What significance does music have throughout the story? What are some ways music affected Gabrielle and her process of healing and remembering?

3. How do you think the story would have changed if Gabrielle had stayed in the city rather than moved to North Dakota?

4. How important is the setting of the ranch in North Dakota?

5. Gabrielle has several opportunities to make friends throughout the book, but she seems to push many people away. Why do you think that is?

6. After Gabrielle went to college, she rarely returned to the ranch. What do you think kept her from going back?

7. What was significant about Gabrielle's "come to Jesus" moment happening in a bathroom, of all places?

8. What is the significance of Gabrielle's relationship with Ian? How does he affect Gabrielle's relationship with Christ?

9. Why do you think the author chose Gabrielle's career path of a veterinarian, and not a doctor?

10. How does Uncle Will use his own experiences and past to help Gabrielle?

11. Describe Gabrielle's walk with God throughout the book. How does it affect her overall outlook on life?

12. How is the theme of forgiveness demonstrated throughout the book? How have you experienced or recognized God's forgiveness in your life?

13. How does Gabrielle mourn the passing of her parents? How is it significant?

14. What is it that finally breaks Gabrielle free to feel joy again? Have you ever had an experience like that?

15. Why did Gabrielle like Bob Dylan music so much? Have you ever had a musician touch your heart the way Dylan touched Gabrielle's?

16. The final sentence of the book reads, "I could hear the clank and rattle of falling chains." What is the significance of this last sentence?